D1795746

IN THIS LIFE

Book One of the Past Life Series

Terri Herman–Ponce

In This Life
Copyright, Terri Herman-Ponce
ISBN-13: 978-0-9911017-0-2
eISBN-13: 978-0-9911017-2-6
First Edition: October 2012
Second Edition: April 2014
Cover: Steven Novak

All rights reserved. No part of this book may be used or reproduced in any manner whatsoever without written permission from the author, except in the case of brief quotations, reviews, and articles.

This book is a work of fiction and any resemblance to persons, living or dead, or places, events, or locales is purely coincidental. The characters are productions of the author's imagination and are used to create a fictitious story.

For Narelle,
my Imzadi and
my Muse

Acknowledgements

There are so many people who helped make this book possible, but in particular:

Harry and Erik – for all the nights and weekends you gave me for writing, editing, reading and marketing, without intrusion. Oh, and for all the Yankees games you let me watch, too. You never complained and I never acknowledged it. I'm acknowledging it now. Thank you for your love and silent encouragement.

The Cherries – for giving me the extra push when this story was just a kernel of an idea so many years ago, especially with chapter one. You may not remember, but I do. It was through you that I learned so much about the craft.

The Guppies – for providing support and letting me vent and just being available with a kind word when I needed it most. I've never met or known a group of writers quite like you.

Sisters in Crime – for all your smarts and experience, all of which I've absorbed over the years. I've learned so much from you.

My fellow CR Sisters – when writing gets hard, you make things fun. I couldn't imagine a day without you in it.

And finally, nothing pleases this writer more than hearing from readers. So keep those emails, web posts, likes and tweets coming. When all is said and done, I write for you.

This is a work of fiction. That means I make stuff up, and sometimes I get things wrong. But in the end, all that matters is that my readers are entertained.

Chapter One

When you've known someone your entire life, there isn't a lot they can say or do that can surprise you anymore. So when David entered the bedroom, tea and toast in hand and a determined look on his face, I knew the words that would come out of his mouth before he even said them.

"No, Lottie. You're not going into work today." And he watched me with an expression that said he knew what I intended to say, too.

"I'm feeling better."

"Really?" He sat down on the king–sized bed and placed the food tray in front of me. "Eat this. All of this. Then we'll talk."

I smelled hot green tea and fresh toast and, for one brief moment, my stomach reminded me that it was empty before rolling over with nausea again.

He sent me a long look. "I figured as much."

I shifted in bed and tried again. "I have a meeting with my boss today, David, plus a new client who's expecting me. I've also got four appointments that I can't walk away from."

"You have the flu and can get your clients sick."

Now he stared me down, aiming for intimidation despite the bare feet, blue jeans, and faded T–shirt. And I saw why the men that David commanded feared and respected him. Powerful stature aside, his green eyes had a way of cutting right through you until you felt compelled to obey his every word.

However, I wasn't one of his men.

I nibbled the toast to prove a point more to me than to David, and my stomach pitched again. David said nothing, probably because he knew better, and I pushed out of bed and headed for the master bathroom. Halfway there, my legs turned rubbery and I knew I'd lost the battle.

Another therapist would have had a field day with my stubbornness.

I leaned against the counter and dropped my head. I felt beaten and fatigued, and uneasiness I'd been experiencing since getting sick prickled at me once again. I couldn't pinpoint the emotion except to call it restlessness, living in a fog that would eventually lift and reveal something with life–altering clarity that I hadn't discovered before. It was an irrational sensation and one I attributed to the flu.

"I'm on leave for the next two weeks," David called out. "Take advantage of that and stay one more day. You know you need the rest and I can take care of you over the weekend until you go back on Monday."

His taking care of me wasn't the issue. The love of my life was an ace in the kitchen and a neat freak with an affectionate bedside manner. I simply wanted to get back on my own two feet, and under my own terms and steam. I grabbed a brush from a drawer and worked it through my hair. As I bent over to get the underside, dizziness followed and I held on to the counter until the room settled down. I drew in a breath, straightened and tried one last time with determined optimism. My hands moved up and down, up and down and then once again.

Two hands became three, then four. I felt a gentle tugging at my head and the weight of something heavy settle on top of it. The hands stroked and pampered, moving from my hair to my face and neck. A noise followed, the sound of a lid removed from a bottle, and a rich, spiced scent spread over the room and over me. I inhaled, long and deep, wanting more. Much, much more.

"Does it meet with your pleasure?" someone asked.

I could not answer. The aroma was too intoxicating and reminded me of him. Of us.

The person spoke my name and repeated the question, and still I could not answer. My name was uttered once more.

"Lottie?"

Hands settled on my shoulders and shook.

"Lottie?"

The aroma started fading away.

"Lottie, can you hear me?" The scent evaporated and I shook my head to clear the remnants of its evocative memories. David stood just behind, a firm grip on arms. "Are you okay?"

"I'll be fine. I just need a moment." I saw his worried expression in the mirror and its intensity surprised me. "What's wrong?"

"Enough of this already." David steered me from the bathroom back to our bed, tucked me in and made sure I felt comfortable. He stood near me for some time and asked, "What happened in there?"

"A little nausea and another dizzy spell." I rubbed my forehead, trying to put a name to what I felt. "Maybe I still have a fever, too."

David touched my forehead, shook his head and sat down beside me. He was studying me now, probing, and trying to see something he didn't see before.

"You were immobile for almost five minutes," he said, tucking my hair behind an ear.

"I think you're exaggerating."

"*Five* minutes."

The restlessness I'd been feeling surged through me again, stronger this time, and I didn't like the way it felt. Something seemed off, and I wasn't sure if it was with David or with me. Remnants of last night's sleep started trickling in, and then a connection clicked into place.

"I had a dream last night and I started remembering it in the bathroom." I closed my eyes, trying to remember more. "I was in a room with a servant who was waiting on me. She was preparing me to meet someone. A boyfriend." No, that wasn't quite right. "A lover."

I felt a tingling uneasiness as I said the word.

"A lover?" David asked.

I opened my eyes, saw David's grin and recognized the bait for what it was.

I grinned back. "The lover wasn't you."

His grin widened and then faded away. "That still doesn't explain your behavior in the bathroom. You looked like a statue."

"I'm tired, David," I said, sliding down under the covers. " The human mind is capable of doing unusual things when a person is under stress, like when they're sick, and the gods only know I've been feeling a lot of that these past few days. Forget about it. It's not a worry."

David paused. "Is that your professional assessment?"

"Yes."

It looked like David wanted to say more but he got up and walked to the windows that overlooked the backyard instead. I wasn't sure what was going through his mind but I knew him well enough to know not to pry. It always backfired whenever I did. So I let him have his moment, toyed with the toast, and then passed on it in favor of some tea. My cell phone rang as soon as I put the mug on the nightstand, and I answered it on the second ring.

"Tough night's sleep, Lottie?" The voice on the other end was male and one I didn't recognize. "You shouldn't tell your boyfriend about your other lovers. Especially those you dream about."

"Who is this?" I asked.

"I'm disappointed you don't recognize me." He laughed, the sound crawling over my skin like a snake over sand. "I'm the man you dreamed about last night."

Chapter Two

The line went dead.

I studied the phone in my hand then looked at David.

"Who was it?" he asked.

"I don't know." Though some part of me, deep down and far out of reach, felt as if maybe I should have known. It wasn't so much the voice that was familiar but a feeling, like a buried emotional memory trying to claw its way to the surface. "But I think he knew me, David."

David stilled. "He?"

A vague image of a man with a deep voice eased in, enveloping me in that rich, spiced scent again. It lingered, reminding me of my dream, and I inhaled deeply to savor it, to hold onto it, until it drifted away. Its absence felt wrong, as if I'd lost something extraordinary and intense. Yet I couldn't explain why.

"Why do you think he knew you?" David asked.

I'd been too wrapped up in the dream to notice David was talking until I realized he had gone silent. With a deep inhalation I refocused and told David about the call.

"I don't know whether to be worried or to write this off as a prank," I said when I finished.

David's gaze swept from me to my phone. Prank calls were typically made from an immature need for attention and threats were usually a manifestation of mental disturbance. But what happened a few minutes ago was neither.

"You sure you didn't recognize the voice?" he asked.

"Positive," I said, shrugging off some lingering doubt. "Something about the caller reminded me of my dream last night. That's all."

David took the phone and cycled through the call history. "No caller ID." He pressed redial and seconds later the bedroom cordless rang.

We both looked at each other as I answered, finding David on the other end of the line.

"How is this possible?" I asked into the receiver.

David took the time to think about it. "Someone either has access to your account or knows how to maneuver around the system." He disconnected the cell phone, took the cordless from my hands and set it back into its charger on the nightstand, and settled down next to me. It felt comforting having him beside me, protective, even if I didn't always need it.

I needed it now.

"So how does he know about my dream?" I asked.

I shuddered and sank further into the bed.

David squeezed my hand in a way that was meant to comfort and tell me that everything was just fine, and dialed another number on my cell.

"Neil, it's David. I need a favor from you." He explained about the call and the redial back to our house. "I want to know who did it and how this happened. See what you can find out and get back to me ASAP."

David disconnected. "Neil is one of my contacts at the phone company. If anyone can get a lead, he can."

This came as no surprise. Ex–Marine turned contract soldier for Professional Recruitment and Operations, a global military corporation known as PROs, David had contacts everywhere.

"Should we call the police?" I asked as he returned to the windows.

He shook his head, a response I pretty much expected. I didn't think the police could do a lot for me either. Give me a troubled teenager, an angry divorcee, or an obsessive–compulsive and I was in my element. But this made me feel vulnerable and exposed. It was as if the dream and the call and the voice unraveled something deep inside.

"David, what happens if Neil doesn't find anything?"

"One step at a time, Lottie." David's voice sounded firm but I heard his doubt, too. Like me, he wanted to write this off as an oddity but neither of us would be able to do that until we found all the answers.

My cell phone rang again. David studied it in his palm, as if he'd forgotten it was there, and checked the display for a caller ID. When he frowned I assumed there was none.

"Want me to do the honors?" he asked.

I shook my head. If I was going to take any kind of control, I had to take the call myself.

The phone rang a third time.

"If it's the guy who called before," David said, handing it over, "don't give him the power. Answer it, but keep him on your turf. Don't let him manipulate you, Lottie."

I sat up and nodded, but was having trouble digesting his instructions. Logically they made sense, but what was happening didn't feel logical. I grabbed the phone, steadied myself, and answered. Paul Cavanaugh, a good friend and colleague from Amrose Counseling Center, was on the other end.

David sat down next to me and whispered. "Who is it?"

I mouthed the answer.

David's jaw clenched. He and Paul tolerated each other at best, and only because of me.

"There's a problem with Logan," Paul said.

"What happened?" I sat up, too quickly, and braced through another surge of dizziness.

David steadied me with a strong hand and sent a stern look.

I ignored it.

"I just got a call from Amrose." Paul's lingering pause meant he had bad news. "Logan's missing. His mother found a suicide note this morning that had been left in his bedroom, but she doesn't know where he is. She couldn't find your number and called Amrose directly, and someone patched her through to Stuart Hanley because you've been out sick. Then Hanley called me."

Hanley served as the director at Sunrise Recovery where Logan, my client, was undergoing drug rehab.

Memories of a teenage client's suicide last year resurfaced, weighing me down with regret and blame. I forgot about my stomach flu and the strange dream and the phone call. All I could see was Deborah's coffin and her distraught mother at the funeral, dressed in black and unable to stand without help because she'd been so heavily sedated.

"Logan's mom wants to meet with you this morning at Amrose," Paul went on. "When I told her you were out sick, she completely lost it. So I called you to see if you could—"

"Of course I'll meet her. I can be there this morning"

David's gaze cut to mine and I mentally prepared for battle.

"I planned to stay home another day, Paul, but I won't do that to Mrs. Reynolds. I can meet her this morning." A quick glance at the digital clock on David's nightstand showed it was just shy of eight–thirty.

"You're not going in," David said.

I waved my hand to shush him and hoped Paul didn't hear. "Can you reschedule my other appointments for today, and let her know that I'll meet her around ten–thirty?"

"Lottie—"

I waved David off again and his shoulders tensed, a warning sign that I might not want to try that again.

"Once she and I are finished," I went on, "I'll head back home." I said the last more to David than to Paul, hoping it was enough to ease the growing tension between us.

"You sure?" Paul asked.

"Definitely."

"Great. I'll let Mrs. Reynolds know."

We disconnected and I pushed off the covers so I could get out of bed. David grabbed my arm, stopping me halfway. He said nothing but he didn't have to. His thoughts were more than evident on his face.

"I have to do this," I told him.

"No, you don't."

"I'm *not* going to let this happen again," I said. "I lost one client already to suicide. I won't lose another." And though hours of my own therapy helped me understand that Deborah's death wasn't my fault, a part of me still had trouble accepting it.

"Can't you have someone else handle Mrs. Reynolds for you?"

"It's not that simple, David," I said. "And please don't order me around and expect me to do something just because you said so."

"I'm not looking to argue about this, Lottie."

"Neither am I but I'm still going."

"You're not well."

"Neither is Mrs. Reynolds!" My voice sounded harsher and louder than I intended, and it startled the both of us.

David looked away, probably balancing his desire to protect me with the need to let me go. He was one of the best people I knew but he also had an edge. It was what made him successful at his job and respected by his men, and occasionally annoying to me.

"This is the least I can do for Mrs. Reynolds," I told him. "Logan is her son and my client and I owe them both."

I stood up, and the minute I got to my feet the room swayed again. David looked at me and sighed out loud, but this time he didn't try to stop me.

I saw his worry just the same. "I'm very well aware that I'm not one hundred percent yet, David, and I promise to be careful."

"I'm working very hard here, you know. I still think this is a mistake."

"I know." And I appreciated it.

David's bright green eyes met mine and the fleeting anger and impatience I felt with him melted away, replaced with something that warmed my heart and filled my soul. He was trying his hardest. The least I could do was to return the favor. So I searched for a compromise and found one.

"Drive me there," I said. "Hang around the office while I meet with Mrs. Reynolds and then drive me back home. This way, if I need help, you'll be there."

He considered me and shook his head, but acceptance only came when he said, "Fine."

I sent him a grateful smile. "Thank you."

He didn't look convinced.

"You can remind me of all the things you disagree with after you bring me back home," I said, leaning down to give him a kiss.

With fingertips to my chin, he gently angled my head so that I was forced to kiss his cheek instead. "I love you, Lottie," he said as he pulled away, "but not your germs."

I made a chicken sound, and David gave me a wide, playful grin.

I slipped out from his hold and, on shaky legs, headed for the bathroom to get ready.

Chapter Three

We took David's SUV and wove through the back roads toward Amrose Counseling Center in Huntington, but I didn't pay attention to the warm, summer morning that surrounded me. I was preoccupied with Logan, preparing myself for every possible conversation I might have with his mother, and each scenario ended with the same desperate outcome. Despite all my training, I didn't know what to say to this woman and I didn't know what to expect from her, especially given what Logan had told me. Much of what he shared about his mother wasn't good, and I had no idea how much of it was true.

We parked under a shady oak and David steadied me as we crossed the treed parking lot. By the time we reached the front door, I was sweating and out of breath. Alicia, the Center's receptionist, gave me a smile that lit up her face as I walked inside. She was the only fifty–something woman I knew who looked more like thirty–something, and for a moment I envied her short silver hair and slender navy pantsuit. She looked fresh and young and vigorous. I felt wilted and beaten and apprehensive. It was a superficial thought, I realized, and one fueled by denial. I simply didn't want to face Mrs. Reynolds or my guilt over Logan.

I blew a kiss to David and heard him make small talk with Alicia as I headed down the muted pastel hallway. Her answering laugh to something he said made me smile. David could banter with the best of them.

I closed the office door and opened a window to let in fresh, July air—something I'd missed while cooped up in bed for three days. The breeze smelled like freshly mowed grass and thick–leaved trees, and I took some time to enjoy its clean simplicity. Another breeze followed, this one carrying a rich, spiced scent that I immediately recognized from my dream.

In the distance I heard laughter and music.

I closed my eyes and followed the happy sounds. Some people were singing. Others were telling jokes and celebrating. And for some reason, I had the feeling that I did not want to be there. I felt out of place in that celebration, and very sad, and was looking for any excuse to leave. Fingertips were touching my chin, coaxing my attention away from my sorrow and back to the festivities. Back to him. He handed me a cup of dark red wine and encouraged me to sip. "You must let go and find your way," he said. "Drink, and let the wine take you where you need to be."

His fingers lingered on me for too long, and he leaned in as if he was going to kiss me.

"Be quiet, Doctor Morgan."

A hand clamped over my mouth and I jumped, startled out of the moment and into Logan's bloodshot, brown–eyed gaze. His flicked a look at the door and then focused back on me, and my heart double–timed with adrenalin and fear. He tightened his grip to make sure I wouldn't run, and I felt tremors vibrate from him into me. He was scared. And high.

"Don't do anything stupid," he said, digging a knife into the underside of my chin.

I swallowed and nodded.

Logan removed his hand from my mouth, slowly, but kept the knife at my throat. He wore a black baseball cap, pulled forward, a black T–shirt, and a pair of designer jeans that I recognized. David once toyed with the idea of buying a pair but couldn't justify spending two hundred dollars on denim. Knowing Logan's background, he probably had on an equally pricey pair of sneakers to match.

I squeezed the armrests on my chair, channeling all the panic down to my fingertips. I was not going to let Logan see that I was scared.

"How did you get in?" I asked.

Logan pointed to the slit screen in the open window. "Couldn't take chances of being seen," he said.

I swallowed, relieved that Logan was alive even though part of me wasn't surprised to see him. Logan was a manipulator and a chameleon and molded every situation to suit his own needs, without regard to how it impacted anyone else. It was behavior many teenagers exhibited, only Logan took it to the extreme. And it was that knowledge that kept me cautious now.

"Does your mother know you're here?" I asked.

Logan moved in closer. His breath smelled of alcohol mixed with something pungent and sour, and I held my breath until my roiling stomach settled down.

"No."

"She's worried. She thinks you're dead."

Logan pulled back and flicked the blade closed with a sharp, disgusted snap. "The only thing my mother cares about is herself."

I kept still and watched him walk toward the light brown

sofa. He sat down and dropped his sneakered feet on top of the wood coffee table, looking like he wanted commiseration and maybe a *poor baby*. He wasn't going to get either.

"She's coming here this morning," I said. "Maybe you should call her and let her know that you're okay."

He blinked his eyes twice, looking like he was fighting the urge to sleep. "Why?"

The question was simple but the answer wasn't. I'd come to the conclusion long ago that Logan and his mother needed family counseling, but neither one of them wanted any part of it.

"It's not like she gives a shit," Logan went on. "She don't need me, what with her rich friends and rich life and rich family." He paused, like he wanted to say something else and wasn't sure how to say it. "You know she's got a new boyfriend now, too?"

He kept watching me, waiting for an answer.

"No."

"Yeah. And get this. I've seen this guy out there where I hang sometimes. He's a player, but she don't see it."

In the year I'd been counseling Logan, I knew of three so-called boyfriends, one of whom had ties to organized crime. The gods only knew what else I didn't know, and how much of it I could believe.

Logan flicked the knife open, closed, then open and closed again. He was buying time.

"Why are you here?" I asked.

He shrugged.

"It seems to me that you're concerned about your mother's welfare."

Logan said nothing.

"Your recognizing her boyfriend as possible trouble indicates an emotional interest in her well being. I'd like to talk about that."

He shrugged again, tugged on the baseball cap and stared at the opposite wall.

"What are you concerned about?"

Logan folded his arms over his chest. "I asked my mom about my dad again last week."

He'd shifted gears but that was okay. It was something I could work with.

"What happened?"

Logan started flicking the knife open and closed again, and I started thinking I should alert someone on staff that he was here. When he flicked the blade closed and slid it into his pocket, I eased back into my chair. I didn't trust Logan, but knowing the knife was no longer easily accessible meant I had regained all the control. I let out a long, quiet breath and felt the knot of tension between my shoulders fade away.

"My mom deposited twenty large into my account so I can take a vacation somewhere. She told me to go away for a few weeks." Logan tugged the baseball cap down further. "I'm so sick of her shit, trying to buy me off all the time. I know why she does it, too. To stop me asking about my dad."

And yet he kept asking about him. And lately more frequently, too.

Logan cursed and sank deeper into the sofa. His body language screamed out a need for love and acceptance and guidance, and the more I studied him and spoke with him, the more I understood his compulsion in finding his father.

Although he never said it outright, I knew he hoped his father would give him what his mother never would or could.

"Do you think faking your death was the best way to deal with this?" I asked.

Logan made a face. "Does it matter?"

"If it doesn't, then why did you do it?"

"Because I want to be on my own and this was the only way I could do it."

"By inventing your suicide?"

He held out his hands like I was a slow learning child. "My mother needs to be taught a lesson. What are you not getting here?"

"How do your actions this morning teach her a lesson?"

Logan leaned forward and rested his elbows on his knees. His knuckles, I noticed, were bloodied and bruised. "What does it matter what I did this morning? Are you my mother now, too? And what if I don't want help? What if I just want to be left alone? Did you ever think of that?"

"Then feel free to leave," I said, motioning to the door.

Logan didn't move.

"Logan, if you believe you're mature enough to be on your own, then why not just do it? Why come back here? Why leave a suicide note for your mother in the first place, when you could just take off and be done with it?"

"I told you already. To teach her a lesson."

And we had come full circle.

I glanced at the clock. We'd been talking for nearly fifteen minutes and Logan's mother was due in another twenty. If I used my time wisely, I might be able to maneuver both him and his mother into my office at the same time. A long shot, but one I hoped for.

And as I thought about the suicide note a little more, another thought came to mind. "Logan, what exactly did your note say?"

For a short second, Logan's large eyes widened with recognition and intelligence, and he grinned. "So Doctor Morgan's gears all finally clicked into place, huh? I didn't leave the bitch a suicide note. I told her I was leaving home and don't come find me."

I remembered the three occasions when Logan ran away from home and ended up in a local rehab center. The most recent time lasted about one month—long–term by Logan's standards—until he ran away from the center, too, only to find his way back into his mother's house where he'd lived for the past several months. He didn't want to be with his mother, and yet he kept returning to her over and over again.

Just like he kept returning to me.

"So your mother misunderstood your note," I told him.

Logan laughed. "She didn't misunderstand it. She lied so she could get to *you*."

The news left me feeling a little dumbfounded. I'd only considered Logan's situation from Logan's point of view because he was my client. Not once did it occur to me that his mother might want help from me, too.

"Hey." Logan snapped his fingers. "You okay? You look kinda somewhere else."

"I'm fine," I said, but there was a sudden rushing noise in my ears and I was having trouble focusing on the conversation. I was hearing the laughter and music again, too, and trying hard to ignore it.

"Yo, doc," he said. "What's the deal?"

Logan's voice sounded muffled and distant, like he was talking to me underwater. He slid over to the end of the couch, closer to me.

"Maybe David needs to make you more soup and tea," he said. "Take you back home and get you under those chocolate brown bed covers. They *are* chocolate brown, right? Isn't that what the package said?"

My eyes went wide and I swallowed down a nervous knot the size of a fist.

"What are you gonna do when he goes away in a couple of weeks?" Through a thin, blurry haze, I thought I saw Logan grin. "Unless my calendar is wrong. He is supposed to go away, right?"

A sick feeling churned in my stomach. One that had nothing to do with the flu. Logan shouldn't have known about David, or anything about our lives.

Logan leaned forward and even though ten feet of carpet and furniture separated us, I felt the walls begin to close in. "See?" he said. "This is what I mean. No one gives me credit for what I can do."

My chest tightened, my throat went dry, and the room swayed and spun around me. I gripped the desk to steady myself. Sweat broke out under my arms and trickled down my back, and the unusual scent I'd smelled since this morning filled the room. I shut my eyes and squeezed the desk harder, trying to calm my breathing so that I didn't pass out.

I felt a presence, nearby and drawing closer. I felt body heat and sensed someone else's attention.

"Do not worry," another voice said, and although I

recognized the voice I did not know where it came from.

I tried answering but my throat swelled and I had trouble taking in air. Something was wrong. The place. The time. The feeling.

Me.

Hands settled on my shoulders, then caressed my hair and my arms and my back. The scent came at me again, and I could not help but breathe it in. It smelled intoxicating and reminded me of something wonderful. Decadent.

I drew in deeper breaths, wanting that scent to engulf me and take me whole. Yet I knew something was wrong. Somewhere, deep down, I sensed it but I could not understand why.

The hands on my body felt different now, no longer attentive but rough. Urgent. A warm breath caressed my face and soft lips pressed against mine. I returned the kiss, wanting more of those lips, more of his body, more of that powerful, exotic scent.

"Lottie?"

My body shook and my surroundings sharpened into focus. I breathed in and tried to find him again, but he was gone. My lips felt warm, tingling with the memory of the kiss that lingered there. An ache grew in my belly and moved lower. I felt empty, wanting him.

A man crouched down in front of me. A man with a handsome face and shocking green eyes that stood out against his dark, near–black hair.

"Lottie?"

Another man was speaking to me now and I heard worry in his voice but did not understand why it was there. I felt so very good and yet he seemed upset.

Two other people stood by his side. One woman with short, silvery hair, and another with locks of gold wrapped tightly atop her head.

I looked at all three and asked, "Who are you?"

Chapter Four

The man looked up at the two women with him and then looked back at me. He sat on his haunches, both of his strong hands clasped on either side of my chair so that I could not get away. He was powerful looking with well–defined muscles, and though his size was intimidating I could see that he was not prepared to hurt me. I may not have been able to run past him but I knew that running would not serve any purpose. In my heart, I knew he was here to protect me.

He blinked and a small smile emerged on his face, but I saw no mirth behind his expression. He seemed confused. More so, he seemed uncomfortable for feeling that way.

"Who are you?" he said, repeating my words. "Not funny."

An odd silence moved in and it took some time for me to understand why. The man wanted me to respond and I felt unsure as to what I should say.

"I did not realize that I was behaving in a manner that amused you."

His gaze narrowed and his expression deepened and intensified, while small worry lines crinkled his forehead and the corners of his eyes. I recognized the expression and understood that it suggested fear, but could not explain why I knew it to be so. I simply knew that he felt it.

I reached out to him and traced my fingertips over his

forehead and down his face. His skin came alive, blazing with heat under my touch. He drew in a deep breath and held it. I dared not pull away, dared not be separated from him and no longer able to feel the fire between us. Yet I knew that if I did not, touching would no longer be enough for either one of us.

I withdrew from him but I longed for more. For a moment, I wondered if he had been the one who kissed me.

"Lottie?" The man spoke just above a whisper but his urgency was clear. "What's wrong?"

"Lottie?" The word felt awkward as it rolled off my tongue. "What is Lottie?"

His face paled and he looked away, as if he were trying to make sense out of something that confused him. It pained me to see him in such discomfort and, against better judgment, I touched his cheek, needing to feel him again.

The heat between us swelled and climaxed and I pulled away with a gasp. The man remained steady and crouched before me, but what I saw in his darkening gaze made my body ache and my flesh burn. Images of the two of us came to mind. Images of a time and a place when we were alone and wrapped in each other, with only our love and our future, and no one else trying to break us apart—

"David?" I said.

I found David staring at me with a look that I recognized but didn't see often. Something was wrong.

"Lottie?"

The way he said my name sounded strange, as if he wasn't sure it was me. David always radiated confidence, even during his most difficult times, but right now I saw only hesitation and doubt.

"Are you feeling okay?" he asked.

"Of course, I'm okay." In fact, I was better than okay. For the first time in days, I felt normal and healthy again, and like the flu had become a long forgotten memory. I was relieved to finally feel better. And hungry.

He looked up at Alicia. "Call 9–1–1. Now."

Alicia hesitated, watching me. Mrs. Reynolds, whom I recognized from a photo Logan once showed me, stood beside her. I wondered when they'd come into the office, and then I wondered where Logan was.

"Logan's alive," I blurted. "Where is he? Have you seen him?"

David fixed Alicia with a hard stare. "Call 9–1–1," he demanded again.

"No, stop. I'm fine, see?" I grabbed his hand and pressed it to my forehead. The fever and nausea were gone and I was raring to go.

I tried standing but David stopped me. "Do you know where you are?" he asked.

"I'm in my office," I said. "And I want to know where Logan is. What did you do with him?"

David drew in a breath and held it.

And I wasn't going to wait anymore. I tugged out of his grip and went to the open window, fingering the tear in the screen and scanning the parking lot for signs that Logan might still be around. I swung around and looked at Mrs. Reynolds.

"Your son is alive," I told her. "He was here, in my office, and we had a conversation about the note he left in his bedroom."

David walked to the window and inspected the damage.

"That screen's been ripped for days," Alicia said. "Since just after you went out on sick leave."

She and David exchanged a look and I didn't like what I saw beneath it.

"My son is *dead*," Mrs. Reynolds insisted, and she turned to David. "Is something wrong with her?"

"David," I said, "I'd like to speak with Mrs. Reynolds. Can you please wait in the reception area with Alicia until we're done?"

Mrs. Reynolds clutched her Louis Vuitton handbag to her chest. "Why are you telling these lies?"

The room swayed again and I heard a distant voice. A woman's voice. I couldn't make out the words but her tone sounded harsh and accusatory. As if I had wronged her.

But no one else in the room was talking.

David was staring at me as if he knew something was wrong and was ready to do something about it.

I didn't give him the chance. "I'd like to explain what I believe is happening," I told Mrs. Reynolds. "I'm not lying and I want to know if you've seen Logan dead or how you can be so certain that he committed suicide."

Mrs. Reynolds took two steps in retreat, her eyes trained on David. "She needs help. I don't know why she's making up such stories—"

"I'm not lying."

Mrs. Reynolds tapped a pointy black Ferragamo on the carpet. "I intend to report your erratic behavior to your director. I will not be patronized. I'm dealing with tremendous loss right now and here you are, telling me I'm wrong."

"Mrs. Reynolds, I assure you—"

"Don't bother," she said. "I've already seen too much."

She marched out of my office as tightly wound as the blonde hair pinned to her head.

I leaned against the wall and stared at the open office door. "I don't understand. This makes no sense. Logan was here," I said, pointing to the sofa he'd just been sitting in, "and we talked. You'd think his mother would be happy to hear the news that he's alive and okay."

David settled onto the edge of my desk, drawing my attention back to him. "Lottie, what's the last thing you remember?"

"Paul."

"I thought you said you remembered Logan."

"No, I mean I want to talk to Paul."

I started for my desk phone but David stopped me. "Okay, assuming what you said is true, w*hen* did you see and talk to Logan?" He held up his own phone and showed me the time. It read ten minutes after eleven.

"That can't be right."

"Should I still get help?" Alicia asked.

I peered past David's shoulder and answered for him. "No."

David let out a long sigh and turned to her. "Alicia, can you leave us alone, please?"

Alicia paused, looking caught between needing to listen to me because she worked with me, and wanting to obey David because he looked more intimidating. After a few moments, she nodded and shut the door after her. David refocused on me and I didn't like what stared back.

"I tried writing off this morning's episode as an anomaly,"

he said. "Something that was the result of the flu and maybe a bad night's sleep. But what am I supposed to think when it happens a second time, Lottie? And worse, when you can't even remember your own name? Or me?"

"It's not uncommon for people to have these types of reactions when they've been very sick, David. You've been through similar situations—"

"I've lost memory because of a concussion, and that was something entirely different. But this?" He motioned between us. "This isn't normal. And you scared the shit out of me."

I could see that I had and that made my heart ache. David was the solid one. The one who always stood firm and always had answers. He was the one who had enough strength for both of us during those times I had none.

Restless, I moved around the office, hoping something along the way would jog things back to life in my head. But the only things that kept coming back were questions about Mrs. Reynolds.

A fragment of a conversation eased into my head. *You are angry with me. Why?*

It was me, speaking to someone else. I knew it as surely as I was standing in my office, but I wasn't talking to David. I was talking to the woman whose voice I heard minutes before. My tone was insistent, even a little sharp, as if I was trying to make her understand something she refused to accept.

"What made you come to my office anyway?" I asked, turning to David, the other conversation fading away.

"Mrs. Reynolds came in while I was waiting for you in reception." David walked over and pretended to show the same interest in my diploma. "Alicia phoned you and when you didn't answer we got worried because you'd been so sick. So we came to your office. We found you alone." He stared at the diploma but I could see he wasn't really looking at it. "You weren't yourself."

I spied the slit in the window screen. The hole, I realized, looked big enough for someone to get into. Or out of.

"He was here," I said again. "Logan's alive and his mother knows it, David. She's playing me but I don't know why."

"Lottie—"

"Please, David, don't. I'm *not* losing my mind."

His features and body language began to soften. I'd managed to get through, if only a little. "I'm helpless here," he said. "In all the years I've known you—and that's been a lot of years—you've never, ever behaved the way I saw you behave this morning."

I pressed my hand to his chest and felt the comforting, rhythmic beat of his heart. He was worried and only trying to help, and that made me want to find a solution that would make us both happy.

"If I have one of these episodes again, I'll see someone. Okay?"

"I want you to see someone now. You're losing moments of your life. You need help."

"David—"

"I don't understand, Lottie. Why are you so afraid?"

"I'm not afraid."

"Then why wait?"

"You don't understand."

He took a step back. "I don't understand? *I* don't *understand?*"

"Why are we arguing?"

"I'm not arguing—"

David stopped when he realized we were.

"I'll talk to Paul," I told him. "If anyone can help, it's him."

The look in David's eyes said everything I needed to know. The last person he wanted me to spend time with was Paul, but Paul was my friend who was also a psychiatrist. A friend who, when things were at their worst between David and me three years ago, had been something more.

David muttered a curse but didn't push the issue. He took my hands in his and steadied me with a probing gaze, peeling away every layer of defenses to get to the heart of me. The part only he understood and knew.

"You're going to make me insane," he said over a heavy sigh. He brushed a hand over my cheek and cupped it, and the heat in his touch seeped into my skin.

I wrapped my hand over his. "Then take comfort in the knowledge that you're shacked up with a therapist who can help you when that time comes."

"It's why I wake up every morning," he said. "Pity I won't be competent enough to know it when it happens."

Chapter Five

The ride home felt strange. David and I sat in awkward silence, and for very different reasons. I knew he was thinking about the two episodes I'd had that morning, and I was thinking about Logan and his mother. I'd called Mrs. Reynolds twice after leaving Amrose but with no luck. I ended up leaving a message but didn't think she'd call back.

As David navigated our SUV up the driveway, I considered how I'd handle my next weekly appointment with Logan, if there were one. I had the feeling he was going to be true to his word and leave for good. And if he did, then what? Would his mother continue to believe he was dead? Would she come after me for telling her what she believed were lies? Or would this all go away with my questions unanswered?

We got out of the SUV and I was aware of David behind me, watching. He let us inside and dropped the keys on the small table in the foyer along with the mail he'd picked up on the way, and went for the kitchen at the back of the house. He didn't say anything but I didn't read his silence as anger. He was troubled, and I let it go. He'd talk to me when he felt ready, and by then I'd probably feel ready, too.

I went to the den that adjoined the kitchen and settled into the leather sofa by the fireplace. I heard the faucet turn on, cabinet doors open and shut, then water filling a teapot. I looked at David and he looked at me.

"I assume you want a mug," he said, holding up my favorite. It was bright yellow with a smiley face. My feel–good mug.

I nodded.

While David worked his way around the kitchen, I turned my attention to the mail. In the pile, I found two solicitations for credits cards with limits large enough to buy a car, along with several trade magazines. I leafed through those and dog–eared articles that I intended to read over the weekend. In the last magazine I found a manila envelope addressed to me in handwritten block print tucked in between the middle pages. I flipped it over. No return address.

I opened the envelope and thought it was empty at first, but after shaking it upside down, strands of long black hair fell onto my lap. Long black hair that looked like mine.

David set the mug on the dark wood coffee table, sat beside me and looked at the strands on my lap. "What's that?"

"I think it's my hair."

I held them up and in one short breath my chest wrenched into a tight knot until I couldn't breathe. I dropped the envelope and the hair on the table and folded my arms over my chest, wanting as much distance from them as possible.

David picked up the hair and studied it without a word. He followed with the envelope, flipping it over and then peering inside.

"No return address," he said, giving it a thorough once–over. "No postmark or postage either. No anything."

"Except my name."

He pressed his lips together, and when his eyes met mine my heart kicked into high gear. We might not have known *who* dropped off the envelope but we knew *how* they did it. They had hand delivered it right to our home.

Though the windows and slider to the back patio were closed and locked, I felt vulnerable and exposed. For a brief, insane moment, my eyes tracked to the bushes and trees that lined the backyard and the inground pool, and I wondered if someone was hiding outside and watching me.

"Do you recognize the handwriting?" David asked.

I kept staring out the slider. "No."

"Any idea why someone would send this to you?"

My eyes flicked to David. "Send me my own hair? No."

"Anyone giving you a hard time at the office?"

I hesitated. "No."

David picked up on my hesitation. "Does it have something to do with Logan?"

There was only so much I could tell him without breaching confidentiality, and I took the time to choose my words carefully. "He knows things, David. Things he shouldn't know. About us."

David said nothing and I knew exactly what his silence meant. He still didn't believe that I'd seen Logan and that he was alive. But he didn't confront me about it and I took that as a good sign. That meant he was still open to possibilities.

David put the envelope and the hair on the coffee table and faced me. "If this hair really came from you, how would someone have been able to get it? And this much of it?"

My hand instinctively went to my head, searching for something that felt out of place. Or missing. I didn't know how someone had managed to get it but, "That's definitely mine," I said. "And you know it, too. Not too many people have hair as long and as straight and as black."

"They're all perfect strands, too," David said. "They look like they've been cut off."

I shuddered over the thought that someone had gotten that close to me without my even knowing it.

"Can you think of any time that you may have fallen asleep with someone else around?" David asked. "Or a time when you blacked out—?"

He stopped talking and I stopped breathing, the both of us thinking the same thing.

"Logan was the only person around when I had that episode at the office today," I said. "But I don't think he did this." Logan was many things but this behavior didn't fit his profile.

David let out a small sigh. "If Logan really is alive, we can't dismiss the possibility. Along with the possibility that we could be overlooking someone else, too."

I looked at the backyard again and the thick wall of bushes around the fence that offered us privacy. "If someone's watching me, what do I do now? Call the police?"

David clasped his hands together and sat in deep, silent thought. "I don't think the cops can or will do anything, Lottie. Unless you know who's after you. And even then, what can we prove?"

I pulled my knees to my chest and wrapped my arms around them. Then David wrapped an arm around me.

"There are a lot of ifs to consider," I said.

"Yes, there are."

His cell phone vibrated. He unclipped it from his jeans, checked caller ID, and answered. The call lasted barely a minute and, when it was over, I felt the muscles in his body contract with tension.

"That was Neil," he said. "He couldn't find anything on the phone call you got this morning. He also couldn't find any reason why the call would route back to our land line."

"So what does that mean?"

"It means that someone's got access to our accounts. Or that they know how to manipulate the phone system. Maybe both." His gaze went back to the envelope on the coffee table and I understood the connection he was making.

"You think the envelope and phone call are linked?"

"Possibly." He punched in a call on his cell and waited for the other end to pick up. "That's why I'm calling Nat. He might be able to find something that Neil overlooked."

This didn't surprise me. Nat was one of David's best friends from childhood and a genius with technology. He was also a contract soldier at PROs.

"Isn't what you're doing considered a misappropriation of PROs' resources?" I asked.

"Not if they're friends who'll cover for me." David's expression soured. It seemed Nat wasn't answering. "Look, I know this won't be easy for you but you don't have a choice."

"Choice with what?"

He left a quick message and hung up. "I'm thinking of having Nat arrange some kind of surveillance on you, so you're covered for the times I can't be with you. Maybe install a tracking device on your Jeep or set up audio in your handbag or some other kind of surveillance for when you're mobile. OnStar maybe. I haven't decided yet."

I pushed away from David. "You can't be serious."

"I know you don't like this, Lottie, but it's for your own good."

"How can a leash be good?"

"This isn't a leash. This is protection. *Your* protection."

I was about to argue but he spoke right over me. "This isn't up for debate. Like it or not, you need to be tailed. My biggest concern is having you watched when I can't be with you, and I trust my men to do that job."

I launched to my feet. "I can take care of myself, David."

David launched up to meet me. "Someone cut off your hair, Lottie. Someone dropped off an envelope in person, right here at our house. Someone called this morning claiming to know what you dreamt about. You've also blanked out twice. And, in case you haven't noticed, all of this happened in the space of five hours."

I'd noticed, all right, but in my denial I was hoping it was just a coincidence. Foolish, I knew, but I couldn't help the reaction. I just wasn't ready to mentally deal with all of it yet.

"I still think you're overreacting," I said. "I'm a grown woman and I can handle myself." I'd done it at the office several times before, and I was prepared to do it again.

"What if someone attacks you in a parking lot?"

"I have my mace."

"What if someone gets into our home and is waiting for you upstairs?"

"I'll run out of the house. Call 9–1–1. Go to a neighbor's."

"What if you have another episode or blank out and someone comes after you then?"

I had no answer.

"Exactly."

His voice sounded sharp, sharper than I'd ever heard before. And it seemed he realized it, too, but before I could react he drew me into a tight embrace and rested his chin on my head. His heart pounded fast and hard and in time with mine, a byproduct of anger, anxiety, and adrenaline.

When the frustration passed and the knotted tension in his body eased, he spoke again. This time with a lot more sympathy. "One of the most important things I learned in the military is survival, Lottie. And the only way a person can survive is to be as prepared as possible and to be as flexible as possible, because whatever you prepare for is going to change the minute you engage. Not knowing what you're up against can make you even more vulnerable, and you have to prepare for that, too."

"I understand."

"Do you?" He pulled away and looked at me, daring me to lie to him. "Do you really know what you're up against?"

I didn't.

"See? And that's what worries me. That's also why I'm suggesting what I'm suggesting."

"Those weren't suggestions," I told him. "Those were orders."

"I know, and I'm sorry." He pressed his lips to my forehead. They felt soft and warm and tempting. "I just want you to take as much control as you can. If you don't and you're caught off–balance or off–guard, you'll make an easier target."

David's phone buzzed again and he held it up so I could see caller ID. It was Nat.

"We have a situation here that I need your help with," he said, pulling away, and he went on to explain about my hair and the note and phone call. He didn't mention anything about either of my blackouts. "I want to set up surveillance on Lottie ASAP. I also want you to check the envelope for prints and do a DNA test on the hair to confirm that it's hers."

David listened as Nat spoke, his eyes occasionally cutting in my direction. I didn't know what to make of his expression because it was so guarded, but I knew that I didn't like that these decisions were being made without my input. Still, I had to admit that David would never tell me how to do my job because he was no expert in psychology. And considering that my safety might have been at risk, I certainly wasn't going to tell him or Nat how to do theirs.

Their conversation went on for another ten minutes as they figured out a plan. I was halfway through my tea when their discussion changed to a completely different topic.

"No," David said. "We'll have to pass on tonight. Lottie had the flu for the past few days, and now with all this other stuff going on I think we should take a rain check."

I launched to my feet. I'd forgotten about Lori's birthday! And we had plans to go out with the two of them to celebrate her thirtieth later that night.

"I know she is, Nat, but Lottie—"

I snagged the cell from David's hand and dodged him when he tried grabbing it back. I was halfway to the kitchen before I realized he wasn't chasing after me.

"Nat, don't listen to him," I said. "Of course we're going out tonight. We wouldn't have it any other way. This is a big night for Lori and we want to be a part of it."

David watched me from the sofa and didn't say a word. Didn't matter. He could fight me all he wanted after I hung up, but we were going out to celebrate.

"When are the reservations?" I asked.

Nat laughed, a deep hearty sound that was always infectious and playful. "Nice to see you're still the boss in that house, Lottie. Reservations are for six–thirty at Dolce's."

"Dolce's! I've never been there but I've heard it's terrific."

"Lori picked it out. The woman's got taste, which is why she picked me."

"Who's watching the kids?"

"Her mom. It's her birthday gift. We're gonna make it a late night, so catch up on your Zs and get into your sexiest. You got that?"

"I got that."

One of Nat's boys screeched in the background. "Gotta go. Now you keep that tough guy in line so I don't have to come over there and kick his ass."

"You bet, Nat. See you later."

I ended the call with a smile on my face. It was something I couldn't help. Nat always had a way of bringing out the happy in me.

"That was sneaky and underhanded," David said, coming to stand by my side.

"I know." I handed him back his phone. "And you deserved it for being so pushy."

David toyed with the phone but seemed preoccupied.

"What is it?" I asked.

He clipped the phone to his jeans and watched me for a long while. "I'd like to say it's nothing but I know you well enough to know you're not going to let it go."

"And?"

He took a few more seconds to finally admit what he'd been thinking. "I'm worried." His voice cracked with the admission and my heart wrenched hearing it. "Worry" wasn't a word often found in his vocabulary. "Still, we can't let that worry get the better of us."

"Which is why we're going out tonight, even though you'd prefer to cancel?"

He nodded.

I slipped my arms around him and rested my head on his chest, wanting comfort and needing reassurance, and not knowing how to find either. If I could forget all of this or make it go away for a little while, I would do it. Then I had an idea.

I looked up at him and the heat in his intense, green eyes made me realize he had the very same idea.

David pulled me to him. His body felt hot, and hard, and I closed my eyes, imagining the wicked, wonderful things we were going to do. "We have an entire afternoon to forget," he said, and his warm breath swept down my neck and over my shoulder, and I shuddered in anticipation.

Then he led me upstairs to our bedroom and made good on his promise.

Chapter Six

By six–thirty, David and I were sliding out of his black SUV and making our way into Dolce's for dinner. We made small talk on the way over, mostly because of an unspoken agreement between us. This night was going to be for us and, more importantly, for Lori. Regardless of the day's events, we didn't intend to spoil a good time.

But that didn't switch David completely into off mode. He watched the valet with wary eyes as he handed over his keys, and he held me close as we walked through the restaurant's front door. By the time we reached the maître d', I wondered if he was going to relax at all during the evening. He looked as tightly wound as an alpha lion ready for the hunt.

Under the guidance of the maître d', we wove through the small restaurant to a quiet table for four in the corner, and I noticed that the darker David's mood, the more attention he received from women. They watched him as he strode through the crowded room, brazen in their admiration of his confidence and looks but cautious of his don't–screw–with–me attitude. One that was well tailored to his dark suit and Italian loafers.

The maître d' held out a chair for me and David took the one to my right. As soon as I settled in, I noticed he'd picked the one seat that had a perfect and complete view of the entire restaurant. Nothing was going to get past him.

"Something wrong?"

David's voice jarred me out of my thoughts.

"No," I said with a smile.

"That doesn't look like a 'no' to me." He smiled, too, but I could tell that it was to coax out the truth rather than to share a comfortable moment.

I weighed what I should say to him and went for, "I want you to relax and have a good time. That's all."

He looked ready to say something then thought better of it, and immediately his strained smile turned into a genuine grin. "Am I that transparent?" Then he quickly added, "Forget I even asked. Stupid question."

I returned the grin.

"Did anyone ever tell you that you're bad for a man's ego?"

"You," I said. "Many times."

He shook his head, picked up the menu and pretended to study it. "There's nothing sacred between us anymore. You're inside my head more than I am."

"Speak for yourself," I said, throwing in just enough suggestiveness to catch his attention.

David's eyes never came up from the menu. "You could have said no this afternoon. I would have found something else to do."

"Yeah. Right." I pretended to study the menu, too.

"Check it out," he said. "They have *seafood fra diavolo*. I haven't had that in ages."

"Are you aiming for humility or discretion? Because neither one suits you."

"And they have king crab, too. Very nice."

"You really want me to believe you'd have tinkered

around the house instead of taking me to our bedroom?"

David peered over the top of his menu, his eyes playful but with a hint of devil lurking just behind. "Yes."

"Liar."

"That's only because you've never said no to me." He placed the menu on his lap and leaned in close enough for me to feel his body heat and smell his rich, inviting cologne. "We can make this a short evening, you know. Go back home and do what we do best."

He trailed his fingers down the zipper of my black dress and heat blazed over my skin and downward. He knew very well how to play me—he always had—and I broke out into a swift, delicious sweat.

David took notice of my flushed skin. "Think Nat and Lori will be upset if we try to rush dinner?"

The urgency in his voice and in his eyes intensified the heat between us. I straightened in my seat, trying for cool and calm and failing horribly.

David kissed my neck, his mouth hot, skilled, and full of passion. He moved to my shoulder, tugged the dress just enough to show bare skin and froze. Just like that, the intimate moment was gone and he pulled away, distracted.

I turned to see what caught his attention and saw a man leaving the restaurant with a woman on his arm, and my breath caught in my throat. "Oh my God! He looks just like Eddie Spellman!"

When I turned back to David, his jaw was clenched and his eyes were narrowed. He was fighting back strong emotion and looking like he might not succeed.

I rested a hand on his thigh. "It's okay, David. What

you're feeling is completely normal, and it's—"

"Please stop psychoanalyzing me," he snapped.

I pulled my hand from him and eased away. "Okay."

He caught the waiter's attention and ordered a bottle of Amarone, trying to pretend nothing was wrong. I'd been expecting a breaking point for more than three weeks already, ever since David and his friends buried Eddie, but David kept fighting the loss just as he was fighting it now. And there was nothing I could do for him.

The waiter returned with the wine, presented it to David, and poured some to sample. David nodded and the waiter filled two glasses and disappeared. Without waiting to toast, David took a long swallow and made short work of the glass.

I studied him and the emotional wall he'd erected between us, wondering if we should leave Dolce's now before Nat and Lori arrived, and before the evening turned into something we might regret later. This was no way for Lori to celebrate her thirtieth and no way for David to grieve over the loss of one of his best friends. I'd been gauging different scenarios and excuses, wondering how we could pull it off without hurting our friends, when David's voice interrupted me.

"We had it all planned out, Lottie. Right down to the smallest detail."

I searched his expression to gauge his mood but his eyes were clouded over by a place far beyond our table and the restaurant. He shook his head over a memory he refused to share and refilled his glass, emptying half of it in two sips. If he realized how quickly and easily the wine went down, he didn't show it. And maybe he didn't care.

I started planning how to get his SUV keys from his

pocket so he couldn't drive home.

He finished the wine, his nostrils flared and his breathing turned shallow and swift.

"Want to leave?" I asked.

He shook his head. "I know what you're thinking. I'll be fine."

But he didn't look fine, and he kept staring out into the distance.

I asked the waiter for a glass of ginger ale, and when he left to get it, the silence between David and me felt as wide and deep as the Sahara where Eddie had died.

David toyed with his glass but didn't pour another refill. "We planned and trained for the Sahara op for months, Lottie." He reached for the bottle of Pellegrino on the table instead. "Did you know temperatures in the Sahara can reach up to one hundred seventy–two degrees?"

"No."

He poured the Pellegrino and I watched the bubbles fizz and burst like tiny exploding stars in his glass. "It didn't get that hot for us, though," he said, "but it was well over one hundred. It was so hot that no matter how much water we drank, it was never enough. We were as dry and dehydrated as the goddamned sand we slogged over."

I pictured David commanding his men on the dunes, ordering them into position for enemy attack. I saw them sweating in desert camouflage, baking under the high desert sun, desperate for cool water. For the sensation of a refreshing spray, sharp and chilling against overheated skin.

In that moment, my skin felt overheated, too. I felt the sun beating down on my body and the sweat rolling down my back.

I imagined how that refreshing water would feel on me. Water that was cool and smelled like clean, crisp linen. The scent of something sweet passed by and I recognized the aroma right away. Honeyed figs and roasted lamb. And fragrant, freshly bloomed flowers. Sand was burning at the soles of my feet and I felt immediate regret over taking off my leather sandals and leaving them further down the banks of the river. I heard someone laugh then, just as a sharp spray of water pelted my body. It was a teenage boy, and he stood waist deep in the river, splashing me and teasing me into joining him for a swim.

The image faded and David's voice eased back in, and I realized I'd missed almost everything he said. But the feeling behind the image remained, like a memory from when David and I were children.

Only it was one that we hadn't experienced.

"I hate that desert, Lottie." David closed his eyes, battling deep emotion and pain that he refused to release. "Eddie was supposed to be on leave, and I was short a man and I ordered him back to serve. If it wasn't for me, he'd still be alive today."

David opened his eyes and cursed under his breath, and I felt the first hot tears roll down my cheeks. I took his hand to comfort him and a sensation jolted through me, hard and swift. I saw the same teenage boy but now as a man. A man who loved me and wanted to marry me, and who took me to the river at night where we drank stolen wine and made love until morning.

A man who wore a linen military kilt and carried a heavy, jeweled sword.

When I released David's hand, the image disappeared and the sound of a deep bass voice along with a distinctive, bubbly laugh moved in.

Nat and Lori had finally arrived.

Chapter Seven

Professional wrestler came to mind every time I saw Nat Hutchins. At six feet four and two hundred forty pounds with buzz–cut, almost white hair, Nat's muscle–bound body stood out from the crowd. Nature determined his physical characteristics and he looked awkward using them. Sitting, walking, even wearing clothes seemed to come at great expense.

He squeezed himself into the seat next to David, leaving Lori the chair next to mine, and she settled in with uncertainty. Nat may not have noticed they had interrupted something important but she did. She looked at me with questioning eyes and I shook my head, telling her not to ask.

"Hey, man," Nat said, slamming a meaty hand into David's.

David shook it and then kissed Lori on the cheek. "Happy birthday."

"And how does it feel to be thirty?" I asked her.

"Thirty's dirty," she said with a laugh. "So I've decided to stick with twenty–nine."

"If I'd have known she'd do that," Nat said, draping the napkin across his lap, "I'd have treated this year's birthday just like last year's and given Lori another designer handbag. Would have been easier on the wallet."

"Don't even think about it," Lori teased, and her hand

lifted to the fine, gold chain and huge diamond that sparkled on her neck.

"Wow." David leaned in to get a closer look. "I'm impressed."

"That's beautiful, Lori," I told her. "Absolutely exquisite."

"I know." Her face beamed with pride. "Nat picked it out all on his own, too. Can you believe it?"

David's eyebrows rose in surprise. Nat was good at many things but choosing jewelry that Lori liked wasn't one of them, mostly because his taste ran on the bulky side. It wasn't that he wanted to be gaudy or show off. It was just that he never seemed to be able to comprehend that Lori stood a good foot shorter than he did and that her petite frame defined her china doll looks. Even now, with her wispy, blonde hair and floral sundress, she looked breakable, and that made the diamond stand out all the more. But this time Nat's choice worked, and very well.

"You have excellent taste," I told him.

"Of course he does," David said. "He married Lori. Best thing he ever did in his life."

David's voice died and he pursed his lips, as if he'd said the right thing but at the wrong time. He flicked an unsettled glance in my direction that he quickly averted.

Nat seemed to pick up on his discomfort and changed the subject. "So what are you guys drinking?" He picked up the bottle of Amarone and read the label. When he saw that it was half full, he added, "Check that. What *were* you guys drinking?"

"We'll order another one," David said, snagging the waiter's attention.

"I'm so sorry we were late." Lori checked her watch. "I hope you two weren't waiting too long and had to start without us. We try so hard but we just can't seem to get out the door in time anymore."

"It's okay," I said. "It can't be easy when you have three young boys at home. And you really weren't late. David was just a little thirsty."

"Must have been one hell of a thirst," Nat said, putting down the bottle just as the waiter returned with the second one and two more glasses. When he disappeared, Nat hung an arm around the back of Lori's chair, his navy jacket and white shirt stretching tight across his chest. Then he surveyed David's tanned skin. "Looks like your down time's agreeing with you, D–Man. Got some good ole fun in the sun going for your time off?"

David shrugged. "Beach. Fishing. Some hoops."

"What? No golf?"

"Are you kidding?" I said. "David's still paying off all those divots he made last year."

"First time and last time," David said. "And never again."

"Sounds like some good vacation, anyway." Nat poured wine for himself and Lori. "But if it's going so good, why the puss on your face when we walked in? You looked like you were ready to hit someone."

I held my breath because this was the last thing the conversation needed.

"Probably gas." David sent Nat a smile and a look that said *drop it*.

"Gotcha." Nat held up his glass and we toasted to Lori's first anniversary of her twenty–ninth year. When he set his wine back on the table, he said, "I thought maybe Lottie was giving you a hard time over the whole psychological evaluation you need done."

David froze with the wineglass at his lips.

"What evaluation?" I asked.

Nat looked at me then at David. "Oh crap. Tell me you didn't ask her yet."

David put his glass down and shot Nat another look, this one even more impatient. "I didn't ask her yet."

"Ask me what?" I said.

"Hey, don't get bent out of shape over this," Nat said. "It's been, what? Two weeks now? Just how long were you thinking of waiting? You told me the other day that you were going to do this before the weekend."

"Ask me what?" I repeated, tuning into the fact that something significant was going on and I knew nothing about it.

"I didn't ask," David said. "And it's not important."

"You gotta give the brass an answer next *week*," Nat said.

"Nat." Lori rested her hand on top of his. "I don't think this is the time—"

"It's for the new guy who's supposed to join David's team," Nat said, looking at me now. "Eddie Spellman's replacement."

David turned on Nat. "Didn't I just say that this could wait?"

"No. You said that it wasn't important."

David and Nat stared at one another and I held my breath, waiting for the scales to tip in the wrong direction.

"Hey," I said, holding up my glass for another toast. "This

is Lori's birthday, so let's promise not to talk business tonight. Okay?"

Lori lifted her glass, eager to change the subject, but neither David nor Nat responded. I clinked my glass against David and Nat's on the table, hoping to get their attention. Then I had to clink again.

Nat shrugged and David backed off and the four of us toasted the birthday girl a second time. As my glass hit David's, I caught his eye and sent him a silent message.

You're off the hook for now but we're talking about this later.

And later could have taken forever. Dinner turned out to be more fun than I had expected. We talked about movies and books and good wine, and joked about our 'old age' and nosy parents and shows we watched on television. We laughed more loudly than we should have but none of us cared. We were best friends, finding a way to make the most of it.

Three hours later we headed for Nirvana, a nightclub a half hour north of Dolce's. Any thought of David and me ending the night early or alone was long gone. We were having too much fun, and that meant I now had the chance to ask David the one question that had been gnawing at me throughout dinner. For some couples, bringing up a touchy subject on the heels of a great celebration meant a hefty fight. But good food, good wine, and great company always put David at his most receptive, and I intended to take advantage of it.

"Tell me about this evaluation," I said.

Streetlights flickered over David's shadowed features while we headed north on Route 110, and he peeked in the SUV's rear view mirror, most likely to make sure Nat's red

Mustang was still behind. He glanced at me, shook his head and smiled.

"I should have known you weren't going to let this rest until tomorrow."

"You can blame Nat for that."

"I already did but I doubt he noticed." David kept his eyes fixed on the darkened street and passing cars.

"You're probably right. Subtle for Nat is getting hit on the head with a brick."

David stopped at a red light and thought things over. "This guy's name is Galen Briscoe and he's supposed to transfer into my team. I need to know what he's about. What makes him tick."

"See, this is what I don't understand, David." I turned in my seat to face him. "I know PROs has procedures for this kind of thing, and that all new hires have to go through psychological evaluation and profiling."

"Yeah, they do. And Galen was thoroughly vetted by one of our psychiatrists."

"So what's the problem? Why involve me? Better yet, why not tell me to begin with? Nat made it sound like you've been sitting on this for weeks."

"I intended to ask you. But then you got sick and I figured that wasn't the time."

"I appreciate the thought, but you still had the entire week before I got sick to say something."

The light turned green, David's foot went to the accelerator and the SUV took off.

"Too close to Eddie's funeral." David's abruptness made it sound like he wanted to shut the conversation down. Eddie's death had hurt him, and more than he wanted to admit.

"Discussing Eddie's replacement is too painful for you, and you're not ready. I can understand that."

"The thing is," David said, navigating through a left turn, "I think Galen's file has been doctored so he could gain clearance to join my team. That's why I want your input."

"What makes you think Galen's file has been tampered with?"

We came to another red light and David paused. "It's just a gut feeling I have, like he's hiding something. I can't explain what it is but there's something about this guy that just rubs me the wrong way, and I don't think his file is telling the entire story."

I blew out a long, edgy sigh. "This isn't as easy as it sounds. You know that, right?"

I knew that he did because we'd discussed it before and often enough. Like David's, my career had its rules, too.

"Because of your relationship with me you become a biased party in his evaluation, which means you can't do it."

"Exactly."

"But not if Galen agrees to the eval, right?" David's gaze held mine, the quiet seconds between us broken when Nat honked his horn from behind. The light had turned green. We drove ahead one block and made a left.

"You asked Galen to make an appointment with me?"

"Yes."

"And he agreed?"

"Yes. And the brass at PROs are on–board with it."

I rested an elbow on my door, dropped my head in my hand and watched the bustling nighttime activity as we drove through downtown Huntington. Twenty–somethings crammed at bar entrances, trying to get inside, and couples enjoyed the warm Friday night, strolling hand in hand.

And I was sitting in an SUV, worrying about losing my license to practice psychology.

"A doctor sees a doctor when they're sick, right? And a therapist sees a therapist when they need help," David said. "Just because Galen was evaluated internally doesn't mean he can't seek guidance externally. I've been stitched up by PROs' physicians dozens of times, Lottie, but I still see my own doctor for everything else. This isn't as out of the ordinary as you might think."

We pulled up behind a line of cars waiting to turn into Nirvana's parking lot. David clicked on his blinker, rested his arm over the steering wheel, and gave me his complete attention.

"Galen wants to serve with me and he's willing to do what it takes to get what he wants. And PROs just wants to make sure this is the right decision for all of us. A decision that's ultimately mine."

"So why do I still feel like something here is wrong?"

David stroked my cheek and cupped my chin in his hand. "I trust you above everyone else in this world. And if you give me a good reason to invalidate Galen, that's all I need to do so."

"And if I don't?"

"Then I guess my gut feeling was wrong."

My stomach flip–flopped over the thought. Instinct was a very powerful component of the human psyche. It was what often fueled our fight–or–flight response and what helped our species survive through the millennia. It was also what made me feel pressured now.

David pulled the SUV up to Nirvana's parking attendant and keyed off the ignition. "Will you do it?" he asked.

I nodded even though I still wasn't sure. "Yes. I'll see Galen on Monday."

He kissed my cheek and got out of the truck, happy. But I wasn't. I hadn't been kidding when I told David that something about this felt wrong. Like David, my gut instinct was humming on this one, too.

The problem was that I couldn't figure out why.

Chapter Eight

Lori and Nat followed us inside Nirvana, a brand new nightclub that throbbed with colored lights, bass music, and pulsating bodies. The four of us circled the darkened area surrounding the crowded dance floor, bumping into patrons and cutting off conversations until we found an empty corner near the back. It had no tables or chairs but we didn't care. Real estate was at a premium at Nirvana, and we were lucky to have found the spot.

David and Nat started talking about the Yankees season and Lori gave me a familiar look and a shrug. I knew what it meant. She wanted to do girl talk and the secondary bar we passed to get to the dance floor would be perfect for it. I told David that we were going for a drink and that we'd return right after, and he sent me off with a kiss and a reminder to keep my promise.

Lori and I elbowed our way through the crowd, squeezed through the heavy glass doors that opened to the other bar and found two empty stools off to the right. The bartender, a guy who looked near thirty and had a blonde ponytail and four gold hoop earrings, hopped on our order. Chardonnay for Lori. Diet Coke for me.

The bar was smaller than the main one near the dance floor, but it was the perfect spot to catch a breather or cool down or have conversation without shouting over loud music.

It carried a Manhattan appeal with a glittering black granite bar, leather and brushed chrome stools, and rows of multi–colored glasses that hung from overhead, brushed chrome racks. I watched the bartender tend to our order and felt Lori's gaze settle on me. I dropped a twenty on the bar to settle the bill and looked at her.

"Here's to your birthday," I said, raising my glass to hers. "And to many, many more happy ones."

We clinked and sipped and the bartender tossed an empty bottle under the counter. Lori winced when it clattered against the other empties in the bin.

"Are you and David okay?" she asked, swiveling toward me. "He didn't look right when Nat and I got to the restaurant. I thought maybe we interrupted something."

The patrons at the bar cheered and high fived when the Yankees hit a single to tie the game.

"He's having a hard time dealing with Eddie's death," I said. "That's all it was."

The crowd cheered again when the Yankees got another base runner, and the cheering grew louder when the next batter homered in the winning runs. The guy next to me whistled, and the sharp sound cut through my ears and into my brain, and then the earth shifted underneath me. I grabbed the bar to steady myself and saw Lori's mouth move but couldn't hear a single word she was saying. I only heard the cheering and the applause.

And a group of women singing.

I scanned the bar again but was no longer looking at the people watching the game. Instead, naked women were dancing across a blue and yellow tiled floor, kicking up canna lilies that were strewn across it as they shook sistrums and sang. I was at a celebration but did not feel like celebrating.

As I watched the dancers, I felt him move in next to me. I felt his heat and smelled the spicy scent I had come to associate only with him. He offered a cup of wine with three lotus petals floating on top, the outer edges of their bright blue color stained a deeper shade of red. He held his own cup and his eyes met mine, and in his gaze I saw an unspoken promise of what was to come.

He sipped the wine and licked his lips and I found myself doing the same, unable to deny the need to admire the beauty of his mouth and the daring in his eyes.

"Lottie?" Lori grabbed my arm. "Are you okay?"

The dancers disappeared and I found Lori looking at me. I nodded and attempted a smile. "I'm fine."

"I told Nat we should have postponed dinner, but he insisted you were feeling better." She took my soda and placed it on the bar next to her empty wine glass. "We should go home."

"No. This is your night. I'll be fine."

I looked around the bar, trying to ground myself back to the here and now. I noticed a few couples but mostly saw women checking out men and men canvassing for women. I watched a young brunette twirl her curly hair around a finger while she talked to an older man in a suit. A guy in jeans and a denim jacket edged up to a blonde woman also wearing jeans and a denim jacket. He offered to buy her a drink. The man next to them sat alone and was watching me.

The muted lighting shadowed his features but I could see his dark gaze pinned to mine. He had short brown hair that framed a lean face and striking brown eyes. He also seemed familiar.

"You look pale, Lottie." Lori tugged on my dress. "Are you even listening to me?"

"Yes."

I felt Lori's hands on my shoulders, trying to guide me away from the bar, but I couldn't sever the hold the mysterious man had on me. He sipped his beer, not once breaking his gaze, and when he placed the bottle on the bar, one corner of his mouth eased up into a knowing grin.

As if he had a secret.

A sultry, spiced scent consumed me and I inhaled deeply. Its warmth radiated over my skin, my body, my spirit, penetrating deeper still. I heard a deep voice and felt a hot, whispering breath against my neck and ear.

"Drink," he said, encouraging the cup of wine to my mouth. "And let it take you where you need to be."

When he pulled away, I felt chilled from his absence. I wanted him near me. With me. And yet I could not persuade myself to follow through. There was too much on my mind, and too much right and wrong to be weighed.

He sipped from his own cup, his eyes never wavering from mine. When he was almost done, he surveyed my mood and said, "He is still very much alive in you, but you must let go." He placed his palm over my aching heart, and my flesh came alive under his fiery touch.

"This is wrong," I said, though I did not quite believe it. And, looking into his eyes, I knew he did not believe it either.

With a shaking hand, I brought the wine to my lips, closed my eyes, and drank.

And then everything went black.

Chapter Nine

When I opened my eyes, I was blinded by light. On instinct, I threw an arm over my face and pain fired down to my fingers, followed by a burning, pinching sensation at the bend of my elbow.

"You might want to take it easy," a soft voice said.

It was David.

"No need to rush. Just take your time."

My eyes fluttered open and I tried adjusting to the brightness surrounding me. In the space of several seconds, I realized I was in a hospital room on a skimpy, thin bed, wearing a skimpy, thin hospital gown, tethered to monitors and IV drips. The bed gave way when David sat next to me and dropped a kiss on my forehead.

"How are you feeling?" he asked, brushing hair from my face.

"Water," I rasped over a dry throat. "Need water."

A small rollaway table stood nearby and he poured water from a pink plastic pitcher into a paper cup and handed it over. My hand couldn't coordinate with my brain and I spilled half on my blanket. David helped hold it to my lips, and his features came into focus as I downed it in one gulp. The top button of his shirt was undone and his tie had been pulled askew. Dark, thick stubble covered his cheeks and chin, and his eyes looked bloodshot and weary from fatigue.

"Where am I?" I asked, handing David the empty cup and pointing to the pitcher for more.

He poured a refill and watched me drink. "Northside General."

"What happened?"

"I wanted to ask you that very thing myself," another voice said.

I looked up and saw a redheaded doctor standing at the foot of my bed. She retrieved a chart from the footboard and her nameplate read Dr. Simonetti.

"You gave David here a very big scare." She sent me a comforting smile that showed perfect teeth nearly as white as her coat. "How are you feeling?"

"Fine, but a little groggy." I tried sitting up but couldn't do it, and Dr. Simonetti adjusted my bed with a remote.

"I'm not surprised," she said. "You've been out for nearly twelve hours."

"Twelve hours!" Panicked, I searched for a clock. "What time is it?"

David checked his watch. "Almost eleven."

I stared at the ceiling, trying hard to remember the last half day but everything came up empty. "Have I been here the whole time?"

My question was directed at Dr. Simonetti but David answered instead. "Yes."

"Doing what?" I blurted, and I regretted asking the question because I wasn't sure I wanted to hear the answer.

This time David said nothing and Dr. Simonetti pulled up a metal chair and sat down on my left. She remained quiet for a moment, and her hesitation turned my panic into full–blown terror. Doctors only paused when they had something bad to say.

"You arrived last night at approximately eleven in a state that mimicked coma but that we eventually determined as a deep sleep. We ran a series of tests to find the cause but they all came back either negative or normal. It was as if your body had shut down so that it could replenish or repair, perhaps from your recent illness, but we couldn't find any other specific reason why." The comforting smile returned. "You're in perfect health, Lottie. Better than most patients I see."

"I don't understand."

"Maybe we should start at the beginning. That may help us all better understand." Dr. Simonetti placed my chart off to the side. "What's the last thing you remember?"

That particular moment came rushing back, hard and fast. It felt as if I'd just been at Nirvana and hadn't lost twelve hours of my life. I told her about dinner and dancing, and that Lori and I spent time at the bar talking.

"Did anything unusual happen prior to your episode? Something that might have triggered your response?"

"No, not that I can think of. We were at the bar for maybe twenty minutes."

"Did you eat or drink anything you normally wouldn't at any point during the night?"

I shook my head.

"Did you feel angry or upset by anything during your conversation with Lori?"

I hesitated.

"What is it?" David asked.

I didn't answer because it was a conversation that I

couldn't bring up now. Not with a stranger in the room.

"Lottie?" David's voice deepened. "What happened?"

I closed my eyes and let the memory take me. "A scent," I said, and I had an odd sensation of feeling bereft of something intimate, and maybe even important. "An intensely exotic scent."

I inhaled, trying to find that powerful aroma again, but I couldn't recreate it no matter how hard I tried. Frustrated, I let out the breath, opened my eyes and focused back on where I was.

"Was it a perfume or cologne?" Dr. Simonetti asked.

"Neither." I was surprised by the frustration and disappointment I heard in my voice. While I couldn't tell them what it was, I couldn't tell them what it wasn't either. "But I do know that I smelled it just after I made eye contact with a man on the other side of the bar." I looked at David. "I think that's when I passed out."

David's eyes narrowed. "Did you know him?"

"He seemed familiar somehow but I don't know from where."

"Work? Gym? Volleyball?"

"I don't know, David. I really don't."

"Did he come near you?"

"No."

"Speak to you?"

"No."

"Did Lori recognize him?"

"I don't think she even knew he was looking at me."

"Or that you were looking at him," David said, and there was a strange quality to his voice that I didn't expect. Not quite jealousy but something close to it.

Dr. Simonetti stood up, hung my chart on the footboard, and turned to me. "Well, the good news is that you're cleared for release. For the record, I consider last night to be an isolated syncopal episode—a fancy term for fainting—that was brought on by the physical stress of a previous illness, a crowded bar and maybe pushing yourself too soon and too fast. I'd suggest that, in the future, you give your body the rest it needs after you get sick. I'm going to write a prescription for bed rest for the balance of the weekend and complete your paperwork so you can get out of here by noon. Sound good?"

I nodded.

"Feel better." She looked at David. "Take care of Lottie and make sure she rests."

David nodded, too.

When the door closed behind her, I looked at David. "You told her about my episodes."

"Yep." David tugged the loosened tie from his neck and shoved it into the breast pocket of his jacket. "She seems to think it's related to your flu." Before I could say *I told you so* he added, "And I don't believe her either."

I frowned.

"Did it happen again last night at the bar?"

I didn't want to tell him because I didn't want to fight about it. I also didn't want to worry David more than he already was.

With fingers to my chin, David coaxed my gaze back on him. "We made a promise, Lottie."

The promise was to never lie to each other again. About three years ago, David and I broke up for nearly a year and it was a breakup caused mostly by lies. It was a horrible time for the both of us and one we never wanted to live through again. When we reconciled, we made the promise to always tell the truth, and we swore to live by it forever.

"It was a small memory this time," I told him. "But I can't place from where, David. It links to the others I've had but I'm not sure how."

"What kind of memory?"

I didn't know because only feelings remained. Fragments of very intense, very passionate feelings combined with a lingering sensation of guilt.

"This is three times in a little more than a day, Lottie. And you promised me that if you had another episode, you'd see a professional."

"I know."

"And?"

I blew out a breath, feeling rushed into the decision. But, a promise was a promise and I owed David that much. "I'll see Paul when I go back to work on Monday."

"No." David shook his head. "You and Paul have a history. I think Denise Rivera would be better. She's the best psychiatrist at PROs and if anyone can help you get to the bottom of this, it's her. I trust her implicitly. She's helped me in the past and I know she can help you, too."

Meaning, he didn't trust Paul.

"Paul can be very objective," I said. "He's who I go to when I can't talk to you and he's also a very good friend."

"And he's biased and too close to you. And you also have to consider Deborah's suicide last year and the fact that she was also Paul's niece—"

David stopped when he realized he'd dredged up the wrong memory at the wrong time. "I'm sorry," he said. "I know how hard it's been for you to deal with what happened to her, but you have to think about Paul's bias. See Denise instead. For me." He paused. "Please."

"I'll think about it."

"You promised, Lottie. You said if it happened again—"

"I know, but this is different."

"It's not different at all. If anything, this is getting worse."

Frustrated, David turned away and pretended to be interested in a flock of small birds circling an evergreen outside the room's window. I watched along with him, using the time and the silence to let the strain between us lose steam.

"Doctor Simonetti was right about what she said before." David kept studying the birds. "You scared the hell out of me last night."

I watched his brooding profile and felt the tension in his body vibrate between us, and realized he was only trying to do right by me because he loved me.

"I'm sorry," I said.

He turned and his eyes searched mine. Penetrating, determined eyes that were trying their damnedest to conceal doubt and concern, and that were shadowed by exhaustion. He'd been through too much since last night and was having a hard time handling it. In fact, the both of us were.

I shifted and patted the empty space beside me in the bed. David shrugged off his suit jacket and kicked off his shoes, eased in and spooned me from behind. He felt warm and strong and sure, and I watched the clock tick away the minutes while the tension in David's body eased and exhaustion drew him into slumber.

An alarm sounded outside the door and a torrent of voices followed, responding to an emergency that needed attention. David tightened his hold and snuggled in closer, murmuring something about not wanting to lose me again. His breath felt warm and soothing against my skin, his arms powerful around my body. I let myself relax with him and, for the first time in days, felt my lingering edginess recede. I closed my eyes and started drifting off with him, and in that twilight sleep I saw shimmering gold linen and bright blue skies, and smelled sweet lilies and cinnamon spiced wine, and felt another man's body on top of mine. I felt the depth of his love, sensed the darkness of betrayal, and watched the sharp glint of a sword arcing down in a final, decisive blow.

I jerked awake, heart hammering and sweating, clutching the sheets with the sensation of the world slipping out from underneath me. Something was out there, outside of my control, shifting and changing direction.

And it felt like death.

Chapter Ten

"I hung with Neil from the phone company while you were at the hospital and guess what we found?"

Nat sat slouched in a saddle colored leather chair in my den, both legs outstretched and crossed at his booted ankles. He looked comfortable there despite the tight blue jeans and T–shirt. Then again, I couldn't remember a time Nat didn't look comfortable in our house because he'd practically made it his second home ever since David and I moved in two years ago.

"We found a transmitter packaged all neat and pretty at the telephone pole down your block."

This caught David's attention and he went still. "So that's why the call to Lottie's cell phone the other morning looked like it originated from here."

"Yup. Someone's been messing with your phone lines."

"Which means we've been tapped," David said.

Nat pointed his finger and pulled an imaginary trigger. "Exactamundo."

"Dinner is just about ready," Lori called out from the kitchen. She ducked into the oven and poked at her lasagna with a fork, and my stomach growled. It had been almost a full day since I last ate a decent meal.

"Were you able to trace the call?" David asked.

"Nope. Damned thing was pretty sophisticated and had a heartbeat."

"What's a heartbeat?" I asked.

David looked at me. "It basically means that someone inserted a device into our phone line that, if tinkered with or removed, would delete any programming associated with it."

"So," Nat added, "we'd have no way of finding who went to all the trouble."

I looked from Nat to David, confused.

"The heartbeat sends a signal to the person doing the tapping," David explained. "Mess with the heartbeat, as Nat and the phone company unknowingly did when they checked the tap earlier, and the man who called you quickly knew someone was snooping around. And the deleted programming guarantees that no one can ever track back to him and what he was doing."

"So what does this all mean?" I asked.

David paused. "It means that this guy's been spooked and will probably change tactics now."

"Tactics?"

Lori set plates, forks, knives and napkins on the large coffee table between us and went back to the kitchen. David's eyes tracked her as she walked away and I wondered what caught his attention.

"Tactics designed to continue to get your attention or scare you," he said, turning back to me.

"Or something more," Nat said.

"We don't know that, Nat."

"I don't understand." I got up, went to the slider and leaned my head against the glass so I could look outside. It was another beautiful July day, bright and sunny and warm, but I couldn't enjoy it. I felt trapped and scared and I wanted answers. Now.

I inhaled and exhaled long and slow, trying to calm down, but it wasn't working. Someone was out there, watching me. For all I knew, they were in the backyard, watching me right now.

Movement near the deep end of the inground pool drew my attention away from the conversation. The tall, wild grasses that framed the diving board and waterfall moved, went still, then moved again. My heart stopped. A breeze blew past and the lofty yellow and green stalks quivered, and then someone with blonde hair slipped deeper inside the shrubs.

Another breeze blew through, this one strong enough to bend the grasses at a sharp angle. No one was there. I'd only imagined it.

"I'll try it another way," David said. "A telecommunication line can—"

"That's not what I mean," I said. "What I mean is, why me?"

"I'm going for blunt here," Nat said, "but if we knew that answer we'd probably already have this solved, wouldn't we?"

I closed my eyes, disappointed.

I felt David's warmth move in from behind, and he wrapped his arms around me and pulled me in close. "What is it I always say to you when things get tough?" His voice was just above a whisper but he sounded strong and sure and confident and everything I wanted to be at that moment.

I sighed. "This situation is more than just tough, David. I'm a psychologist and even I don't have any words to explain this."

"Humor me."

I turned and looked up at him. "Fine," I said, reciting David's words from memory, which was easy enough to do because I'd heard them so often I'd lost count. "If your enemy is in superior strength, evade him. If your opponent is temperamental, seek to irritate him. Pretend to be weak, that he may grow arrogant."

"Ah," Nat said. "Sun Tzu's *The Art of War*. I love that book."

"That and the *Kama Sutra*," Lori said.

David shook his head and smiled but I could see the edginess behind it. "And the point of all that is?"

"To prepare."

"And to be clever." He tapped a finger to my forehead. "And to remember that once a plan is set in motion, you have to expect to change it once you engage."

I eased out of David's embrace and watched Lori set dinner on the coffee table. "You make it sound simple, David."

"In some ways it *is* simple. Preparation and practicality are two things that make a difference, Lottie."

"That," Nat said, holding up a forkful of lasagna to make his point, "and knowing when to fight."

Lori settled down on the floor next to her husband. "But this isn't war."

"Isn't it?" Nat asked.

"Not even close!" Lori stared at Nat like he'd lost all sense of reality. "Does it look like Lottie's in a battlefield and dressed in camouflage? Is she aiming a gun or throwing a grenade?"

"Wars and battles come in all shapes and sizes."

"If there's an opponent of any kind," David said, "then it's a war."

Not to me it wasn't, but I wasn't about to argue the point because this was the one big difference between David and me. He saw life as a series of battles to be fought in order to grow stronger intellectually and physically. I saw life as a learning experience so that you grew stronger emotionally and spiritually.

Lori scooped out three helpings of dinner for herself, David, and me. Nat dug in for seconds. I sank into the sofa, cross–legged, and toyed with my food.

"Aren't you going to eat?" Lori asked.

"I guess." But eating wasn't really on my mind anymore. My stomach was in knots and seeing David so preoccupied bothered me. He commanded ops in far more threatening situations than this, but this was new territory even for him.

"Something just occurred to me," he said. "I don't think the guy who called yesterday morning knew about your dream. No one can read minds, much as many people like to think they can. Now that I know our phone's been tapped, I'm thinking that this guy heard our conversation and twisted it in his favor to make it seem like he did."

"Meaning what?" I asked. "Someone's eavesdropping?"

"One step ahead of you, D–Man, and that's gonna be a big fat no." Nat downed another forkful of lasagna. "When I found out about the phone tap, I got two men from PROs to sweep the house and your cars this morning. Seemed to make sense to do it, given what we knew. Anyway, we didn't do a complete job but we were pretty thorough, and what we searched came up a big nada."

"You think our house was bugged?"

"Yep. But far as I can tell, it wasn't."

And we were back to square one. "Then how did the caller know what I'd been dreaming about? It doesn't make any sense."

David went back to studying the yard, and I wondered if he was searching the trees and bushes for a stalker like I'd been. "Good question," he said.

I pushed my plate away. "I'm with you on this one, David. People can't read minds. We *must* be missing something."

Lori picked up my plate and handed it back, daring me to deny myself a good meal. I took a bite but, like the beautiful day outdoors, just couldn't enjoy it.

"I saw a man on one of those morning shows that could do it," Lori said, serving Nat his third plateful. "Read minds, that is. This is going back a few months and I don't remember details, but I do remember that he was really good at it."

The rest of us paused and stared at her.

"I swear," she said. "It's true. He's some big shot in the mind–reading world."

"They have a *world*?" Nat asked.

Lori slapped Nat with a napkin. "You know what I mean. It's not like he's the only one who does it. But he's an expert at it."

"Mind reading is a farce, just like tarot cards and fortunetelling. It's a means for people to fraud money off other people." David joined us at the table and sat down. "I'm sure the guy was entertaining, but all you need is a little experience with people and some psychology to make it look like you can do those things."

Lori made a face like she didn't agree. "He knew things

about the audience, David. Personal things that no one else could possibly know, and it was scary to watch. If that's not mind reading, I don't know what is."

"Lottie's a psychologist and she's experienced with people," Nat said. "Do you think you could mind read?"

Once, I went to a mind reader with friends at a college carnival. And she'd gotten everything about me all wrong. "That isn't what this conversation is about," I said. "This is about finding out how someone could know what I dreamt about. Or why someone would tap my phone."

"And how he got access," David added.

"Well," Lori said, "he knows you from somewhere, obviously. People don't do things like this unless there's a reason. Or a connection."

"Crap." Nat wiped his hands with a napkin and dropped it onto his empty plate. "I almost forgot. I shipped the envelope and hair off to our buddies in forensics this morning. Put a rush on it, too."

"Good." David dug into his meal. "Maybe that'll start giving us what we need."

"It's still going to take some time to get results," Nat said. "But at least we've got it moving."

The doorbell rang as David scooped up another forkful. He looked at me and hesitated. "You expecting anyone?"

"No."

"Neither am I."

He went to the foyer and the front door, and another man's voice answered David's. David returned with a large bouquet of unusual, light blue flowers nestled in a clear vase and tied with a white bow.

"They're for you."

David set the bouquet on the coffee table in front of me and stared at it, hands on hips.

"Oh wow. They're beautiful!" I leaned in and inhaled, and found them as fragrant as they were striking. Warm and sweet and earthy. "Thank you, David. These are so lovely."

"They're not from me."

I looked up at David, a little too quickly, and for a moment felt woozy. David tugged off the card and read out loud what had been written.

I was very worried when I heard you went to the hospital. But you should be more careful next time. Next time, someone might not be there to help you.

He checked for a signature and didn't find one. "No name. No nothing."

"Except for this," Nat said.

He reached into the flowers and pulled out more strands of my hair.

Chapter Eleven

"I'm calling the police."

Before I could pick up the phone, David had my hand. "Think this through, first."

"What's to think about?" I tugged away from him, filled with a sudden, compelling urge to smell the flowers again. I should have felt revolted by them but they had captured and held my attention and I couldn't let go. They seemed familiar and I wanted to remember from where.

Nat stood up and joined us. "David's right about this." He took me by the shoulders and I pulled away from him, too. "The cops are going to fire questions at you, and you need to be prepared to answer them, Lottie."

"So let them ask questions," I said. "Isn't that the point?"

"It's not that simple."

"Why not?" I sank into the sofa and toyed with the delightful, blue and white blooms. In a deeper part of my mind, I remembered wearing them in my hair, and seeing them strewn across blue and green and yellow tiled floors and festively ribboned over massive granite columns.

And I remembered them floating in a cup of red wine.

"We're not trying to belittle you," David said. "And we're not trying to tell you what to do. It's just that—" He pushed the flowers away from me. "Are you even listening?"

"Of course I am."

But I couldn't break away from the bouquet. I pulled out one single stem and held it to my nose. Something about the scent made me breathless and aroused.

"What's with you?" David asked.

"Nothing," I said. "These smell wonderful. Want to try?"

I held the bloom to David's nose but he pulled away. "Have you been hitting the wine or my mother's brownies again?"

"Oh come on, David."

"Those flowers may be beautiful, Lottie," Lori said, "but they're creepy. And they need attention."

I shrugged. "Maybe a little water."

"I meant that they need the *police's* attention." The three of us turned to find Lori holding up her cell phone. "I called my uncle's precinct and a car's on its way."

"Why?" Nat asked.

Lori looked at him as if he'd lost his mind. "We need professionals to handle this situation."

"We *are* professionals."

"Police," she reminded him. "We need the police."

"They're going to do jack," Nat fired back.

"Maybe, maybe not, but what happened should be on record." Lori picked up a couple of dishes and handed them to Nat. "So get over it and start cleaning up."

Nat's face reddened but he took the dishes and headed into the kitchen. David hesitated but followed Nat's lead, cleaning up what remained. I smiled as I watched them both load the dishwasher, recognizing that although she wasn't the aggressive type, Lori had managed to pull David's and Nat's need for control right out from under them. When they were out of earshot she leaned to whisper in my ear.

"They're pretty ticked at me right now."

"I know," I said. "And I love it." I twirled the fine, pointed petals against my nose, and Lori hovered a little longer.

"What's the deal with you and those flowers, anyway?" she asked.

"I don't know." I inhaled the bloom and sighed. "They just smell really good." I offered the flower to Lori but she shook her head, too.

"You don't know where they came from," she said. "Don't you think the way you're handling them is a little weird?"

"They just seem familiar to me," I told her. "And I'm trying to remember from where."

Lori grinned. "An old boyfriend?"

I grinned back. "Maybe."

"Who?"

I kept twirling the petals, thinking.

Lori leaned in closer. "Come on, Lottie. Who?"

"I honestly don't know," I whispered, "but the memory's a hot one."

With mischief in her eyes, Lori glanced at David storing leftovers in the freezer. "I'm guessing it's not him."

I shook my head and laughed.

When the doorbell rang, I slipped the bloom back into the vase. David greeted the police and ushered them inside. Officer Jim McKarren, Lori's uncle, strode in first. He was a fit man in his late forties with a wide forehead, brown hair, and eyes as blue as the flowers. A blonde officer who looked twenty years his junior followed. His brass tag read Llewellyn.

"I understand there's been a situation?" Jim looked to Lori

for direction and Lori gestured toward me.

"Yes," I said.

David shoved his hands into his jeans pockets and leaned against the counter that separated the kitchen from the den, shoulders squared and eyes alert.

Jim McKarren sent him a cursory glance and bypassed him in favor of one of the leather chairs near me, taking a quick visual inventory of the den. I wondered if his appraisal came from personal curiosity to see what had changed since his visit last year or from professional training to find something out of place. His eyes never went to the flowers. Llewellyn remained near the fireplace and I had a swift and vivid image of a soldier standing sentry, prepared to defend. Or attack.

"Tell me what happened," Jim said. "Lori claimed that someone was being threatened."

I pointed to the flowers and showed him the card and my hair. "These arrived about a half hour ago, and I don't know who sent them to me."

Jim studied each item for a few minutes and then studied me. "And?"

"The card isn't signed."

"And?"

I remembered the last time Jim and I had a conversation. That one had been short and interrogatory, too.

"And the people who knew I was in the hospital last night didn't send me these flowers," I said. "Someone else did."

"And that makes this delivery a threat?"

"It's not just the delivery," I told Jim. "It's the fact that there's no name on the card and my hair is in the bouquet."

"Did you smell the bouquet after it was delivered?"

"Yes."

"So maybe your hair got stuck there all on its own."

Jim looked at Llewellyn. Though neither showed any emotion during their silent exchange, I knew what Jim was thinking and my heart sank. When David's eyes sought out mine, I understood the corner I'd trapped myself in. I could have told Jim that something similar had happened once already, but then I'd have to tell him everything else. And then I'd have to explain that David was using PROs resources to examine my hair and our phone records and the envelope, and if I did that then the precinct would notify PROs and David's job would be at risk.

Jim turned back to me. "What are you not telling me, Lottie?"

I kept my gaze steady with his. "Nothing. You know everything."

Jim fed me his silence and I recognized the prompt for what it was—an enticement to get me to fill it. It was a powerful motivator and one I used often with clients.

"I just feel like someone's after me and I don't like the feeling," I admitted, and it was the first completely truthful thing I'd said since they arrived. Frustrated, I got up, went to the slider and looked outside once more, searching for anything that would take my mind off my screw–up. The rose bushes, I noticed, needed pruning.

David's voice cut in. "I'm sorry, Jim. Lottie's been having a difficult time with one of her clients and I think she's feeling vulnerable lately because of it. I suspect that's one of the reasons why Lori called you here."

The explanation seemed to pacify Jim. He stood up and

motioned to Llewellyn. "The best thing I can do is investigate the delivery and try to get a name. Other than that," he said, "there's not much else I can do for you."

I told McKarren that I was grateful for their time and Lori gave her uncle a hug. David walked both officers to the front door where the conversation continued a little longer. Lori dropped a kiss on my cheek and offered an "I'm sorry, sweetie" before heading back into the kitchen. I heard the television click on and a baseball game tune in, and through the slider's reflection I watched Nat sit on the sofa and prop his feet on the coffee table next to the flowers. Again, their unique beauty and color drew me in, as I knew I had been drawn to them before.

I felt skilled hands powder me with gold dust and slip a new gold and linen sheath over my body. The hands placed a collar made of gold tubes laced with amethyst and carnelian around my neck, and a braided wig threaded with gold on my head.

"Does it meet with your pleasure?" my servant asked, handing me a mirror.

I did not need the mirror to know that it did, and I nodded my approval.

With one final adjustment to my wig, she urged me to my feet, out into the royal courtyard and to the Great Hall. Trumpets blared, heralding my arrival and my heart soared as I entered the celebration. Garlands made of lilies and lotus hung from the ceilings and wrapped around each sculpted column. Flower petals of blue and green and yellow adorned each table as well as the reed mats beside them. Servant girls tied floral collars of chamomile and green leaf on guests, and empty wine jugs spilled over with blue and white lotus. Women poured wine spiced with cinnamon into cups and others served trays filled with dried fish, figs and dates, thick loaves of bread, and seasoned beef. People ate and drank, women danced and shook sistrums, and music played long into a night that promised future success and eternal happiness.

After a time, in need of fresh air, I excused myself from my table. Although the night was warm it was not uncomfortable and, for once, a cooling breeze blew through. At the edge of the granite balcony, I closed my eyes and relaxed under the gentle wind, allowing the effects of the wine to quiet my senses. I sensed someone move in from behind.

"It is a magnificent night, is it not?"

I did not need to look to know who had joined me. His voice warmed my blood as much as the wine did.

"It is," I said to him.

He nudged my arm and when I opened my eyes he held up two cups of wine, offering me one.

I hesitated. My heart belonged to another man and yet here we stood, alone beneath a dark, moonlit night.

"It is from my vineyard," he said in an attempt to sway my decision.

He offered the cup again and moved in beside me. The wine looked as rich and red as the darkest pomegranate, with three blue lotus petals floating on top. I took the cup but did not drink.

Much to his credit, he did not try to sway me again. "What a remarkable view," he said, taking a sip and then one more. "Everything seems to glow with moonlight. Even the river glitters beneath the stars, as if it is filled with shining jewels."

I nodded but it seemed all I could do. I was having a hard time focusing on the view, the wine, even the night itself. His voice stole every thought from my head and had command over every reaction in my body. But he was not mine. And I could not stay with him here. Alone.

I moved away, needing space. This, whatever this was, felt dangerous and wrong.

He glanced my way, the trace of a grin playing on his lips, the darkness in his eyes drawing me into a place I had never been before. A place that harbored secrets and promised danger.

A place I had to avoid.

I felt a kiss on my cheek and heard a woman's voice once more. "I'll call you tomorrow, okay?"

The den slipped back into view, and the scent of cinnamon wine and fragrant flowers was replaced with robust marinara and spicy oregano. The sounds of song and dance turned into Nat's cheers for the baseball game.

And the dark, beckoning eyes that had aroused and tantalized faded away.

Lori was standing beside me. "Maybe I'll bring dinner again, too. Might as well take advantage while my mother handles the boys for the weekend."

Nat remoted off the television and stood. "And I'll check into the florists because I know the cops will get squat on this."

David returned to the den, alone. "Great idea."

Nat and Lori said their goodbyes and promised to swing by tomorrow, and David finished cleaning up. I stayed by the slider, watching the sun begin to dip in a purpling sky. Water turned on and turned off, plates rattled and the refrigerator pulled open and sealed shut.

A short while later David wrapped his arms around me, his heart beating in time with mine. "You okay?" he asked, dropping a kiss on top of my head.

"Yeah." The evening's first few stars sparkled in the purpling sky. "You were right about me not being ready to talk to the police. I could have handled that better."

I stared into David's eyes. They weren't the dark, secretive eyes I had remembered moments before.

"You look like you need rest," he said. "Maybe you should go upstairs to bed."

I hesitated, wanting to tell him about what I'd seen but I wasn't sure how to put into words what I didn't understand myself. I nodded, kissed him and headed for the foyer and the stairs.

Halfway to the second floor, I sensed David following me.

"What are you doing?" I asked.

We reached the landing and turned down the hall. "I'm going to rest with you."

I stopped him with a hand to his chest, just outside the double doors to our bedroom. "So we're clear here, my definition of rest is not doing anything. Just lying in bed. Maybe even falling asleep."

"No problem," David said, maneuvering me past the threshold. "You can do all those things. As long as you promise to fall asleep afterward and not during."

"And what if I say no?"

David stopped. "Are you?"

I rolled my eyes, sighed out loud and grabbed his hand, leading him further inside. "I'm such a cheap date."

"I wouldn't quite put it in those words," David said, closing the doors behind us. "But it's one of the things I love most about you."

Chapter Twelve

By the time Monday arrived, I was ready to go back to work.

As much as I loved being home with David, I needed to return to some kind of normal life—one that involved getting out of the house and behaving like any other person who had bills to pay and food to put on the table. But the term *normal*, at least right now, came with a big caveat. My handbag, phone, and Jeep had been outfitted with a tracking device, courtesy of Nat. My home security system had been beefed up, courtesy of the central monitoring station. And all questionable external contact, snail mail and phone calls and e–mail included, was going to get the once–over by David. As I fastened my dress and slipped on a pair of sandals, I wondered how long it would take before a watch party would be posted outside my bathroom door, too.

Under other circumstances, the visual would have been funny. I knew David and Nat were doing what they thought was necessary but the idea of having my every move under scrutiny grated on me. I didn't do well with supervision of any type.

I sat on the edge of the bed and sighed, trying to convince myself to get over it because this was important, and for good reason. I hadn't heard back from Jim McKarren yet, but Nat researched flower deliveries into the area and didn't find any that were addressed to my home or me. On top of that, he'd discovered that the flowers—blue lotus, he'd called them— carried a mild psychoactive property that could elicit tranquility in the user, and even heightened mental states or sexual performance when blended as a tea or mixed with wine. Once David heard that, the flowers ended up in the garbage.

While the information made David suspicious it intrigued me, though in a tentative way. In David's mind, everything that had happened since Friday morning was more than just coincidence. And I agreed but with one major difference. I now knew that my episodes were no longer something clinical but something very personal instead. But the bigger question was why everything I kept seeing and feeling seemed to stem from memories that I'd never experienced before in my life.

That's when I made a firm decision to speak to Paul once I got to the office. I scanned my cell phone and discovered that I had a fully booked day including an initial consultation with Galen at nine–thirty. I had thirty minutes blocked out with him, and hoped it would be enough to give David the preliminary evaluation he wanted. Somewhere in between I'd have to figure out how to fit Paul in. And I needed to connect with Mrs. Reynolds, too. I considered phoning her from the office on my lunch hour but realized that caller ID could be an issue if she was truly avoiding me. That also meant my cell phone wasn't an option either, and for the very same reason.

I spied David's cell on his nightstand. His phone was unlisted and, with a ten–minute cushion left before I needed to leave for work, I figured I had nothing to lose. I searched through my contacts on my own cell, found Mrs. Reynolds's number and dialed. She picked up just before I thought I'd hit voicemail.

"Hi, Mrs. Reynolds. This is Doctor Morgan from Amrose."

"I want you to leave me alone—"

"Please don't hang up. I only want to talk."

I kept my voice neutral with the hope that she'd stay on the line, at least for a short while, and knew I'd succeeded when silence greeted me on the other end.

"I want to apologize for what happened the other day at my office," I said. "I feel very badly about the way our conversation ended."

"My son is gone, Doctor Morgan. What is there for us to talk about now?"

"Gone?" I asked, catching her slip–up. "Or dead?"

Mrs. Reynolds hung up.

I stared at David's cell, not surprised by her reaction. We both knew that Logan was alive but playing her game seemed the only way for me to get her attention. Still, I felt disappointed. Talking with her was no guarantee of honesty but even her lies would give me clues to work with. Unfortunately, she wasn't giving me much of that, either.

I decided to try her again tomorrow.

I grabbed my handbag, keys, and phone, and headed downstairs to the kitchen. David sat at the table in the dining nook near the other sliding door, tablet in his left hand, coffee mug in the right, dressed in a gray T–shirt and black basketball shorts. He looked up when he heard me walk in and sent me a heart–stopping smile.

"You sure you don't want anything?" he asked, using his coffee mug to point out the bagel on the plate before him.

I shook my head. "I'm good."

He considered me for a moment, put down his mug and his tablet, and came over. When he pulled me in close, I smelled fresh soap and shampoo mixed with my favorite, musky cologne. I snuggled into him, inhaling as much of him as I could.

"I'm going for a long run later and then heading to the gym," he said.

In case something happens and you need to reach me was left unspoken.

"Enjoy it," I said.

David escorted me to the garage and gave me a kiss after I settled into my Jeep, and watched as I pulled out of the driveway. I reached Amrose in twenty minutes, courtesy of thin traffic and plenty of green lights, and found Paul in his office next to mine.

"Have a few minutes?" I asked, poking my head inside his open door.

He peered at me over his computer and waved me in. "For you, any time."

"I need some help," I said, taking the chair opposite his desk. "Guidance, actually."

"I'm all ears." He shoved his laptop aside, giving me full view of tanned arms that were complemented by an even darker tan golf shirt. The color, I noticed, brought out the light brown in his eyes and hair and accented the slivers of gray that were starting to appear on his temples. They were the only hint that Paul had already moved past forty.

"Since you're the expert, what can you tell me about memories? Specifically false memory and episodic memory?"

He leaned forward, interested and intrigued. "Episodic

memory is associated with personal memories and involves sensations and emotions related to a particular place or time. False memory is more of a syndrome. It's usually centered on a traumatic experience, resulting in memories that are factually incorrect but that a person strongly believes."

"Meaning that episodic memory is more accurate?"

"It's not a matter of accuracy in the way you're thinking." Paul leaned back in his office chair, folded his hands behind his head, and stretched out his legs. It was his thinking pose, and one he'd been doing since I met him at Amrose four years ago. "It's more the difference among where and what and when. Episodic memory is re–living an occurrence along with the sensations the memory invokes, but you don't confuse it with your current place and time. You see the memory for what it is—a snapshot into the past."

"And false memory?"

"It's more a distortion of an experience, but it can also be the result of a fantasy that the individual believes is factual."

"Like something that happens in a dream?"

"That's possible, yes." Paul tilted his head and studied me. "Why? Have a client who's exhibiting this behavior?"

"No," I said, getting up and closing the office door. "I am."

I told him everything. From my flu to the phone call and the envelope, to dinner and the bar and the hospital stay that followed. I finished with the flowers and the police, and all the episodes I'd experienced in between, and when I was done I'd shared more with Paul than I had with David.

Paul's lips thinned. "Your episodes," he said, "are the reasons why you're asking me about memory."

I nodded. "Because they *feel* like a memory, Paul, but I'm wondering if this is a false memory. The problem is that it seems very real and that's what's confusing me."

"Do you recognize anyone in these memories? Or any place?"

I let out a small laugh at the question, not because it was funny but because Paul had so readily accepted my experience as something genuine. David didn't, and couldn't, because he relied on facts and tangible evidence to make a decision while Paul relied on incidents and the perceptions behind them.

"I don't recognize anything," I said, sitting the edge of the desk. "But at the same time I do."

"Well, the fact that you're questioning the memory's validity is a good thing. It shows you're not crazy."

"Gee. Thanks."

"I'm serious." He got up and sat on the desk next to me. "If you want to get to the bottom of this, I'd suggest trying not to fight the episode the next time it happens. Go with it and see where it takes you. Try to make a connection between when it occurs and what you're doing at the time it happens, and where you are. You might find an association and answers to your questions."

"What if I can't?"

"If you can't find an association then you can talk to me again."

Paul's gaze met and held mine. A small smile, one that hinted of things we'd done a long time ago, curved up the corners of his mouth. My heart beat slowed, my breathing grew deeper, and in the seconds that passed I remembered just how easy it used to be with Paul. Conversation had always been uncomplicated and time spent together always felt relaxed. There was never a crisis to handle or argument to reconcile. It was simple. Except for the fact that he was married and I was in love with David.

Paul's computer alarm went off, alerting him to his next appointment and breaking the moment between us. He got up, checked the calendar entry and disabled the alarm. When he looked at me again, he was back to professional mode. "By the way, I heard about what happened on Friday with Mrs. Reynolds. Did Logan really show up at your office?"

"Yes," I said, grabbing my handbag and filling him in on those details, too. "I even called her this morning to talk about it."

"What happened?"

"She hung up."

Paul held the door open for me. "Why even bother pursuing her, Lottie? If Logan's alive and she doesn't care that he is, why get involved?"

"I have a feeling she wants to get my attention. Besides, Logan is my client."

"I don't think it's a good idea for you to poke this particular beehive."

"But she lied about Logan. Don't you think that's strange?"

"Lottie, she came after you once and only once. From there, it was you who did the pursuing. If she wants to talk to you, let her come to you on her terms. Same thing with Logan. What you really need to worry about is yourself and whoever's sending those deliveries."

"I guess."

"No guessing because you know it's true."

Past Paul's shoulder and on a bookshelf I saw a photo of him, his brother and his niece, Deborah. Paul followed my gaze and let out a sigh filled with melancholy.

"Deborah would have been eighteen this year," he said. "Such a waste and so much life ahead of her."

I took his hand and squeezed. "I tried doing everything I could for her. You know that, right?"

Paul squeezed back. "I know."

The computer alarm beeped a second time. "I have to go," he said, but he kept holding my hand and a few seconds of unspoken thoughts and unfulfilled promises and what–ifs lingered in between. Then he pulled away and gestured that I should leave.

When I got to my office, I settled in, dug into my bag, and pulled out Galen's profile to review one last time. The file was thick but I kept to the basics. He had been born in Australia and had a sister four years younger. His family moved to Saudi Arabia when he turned three, and then the United States when he turned ten. An IQ of 172 awarded him a high school diploma by the age of fifteen and a Bachelor of Arts in Criminology from John Jay College at seventeen. At nineteen, Galen joined the Marines, became an officer and completed a six–year tour before accepting an honorable discharge. PROs recruited him immediately after and had been his employer ever since, during which time he served in their offices in New York, Japan, and the United Kingdom. The file contained flattering military testimonials, commendations for medals of valor and evaluations from PROs' psychiatrists attesting to Galen's emotional stability and mental health.

And, for some reason, David didn't trust him.

I was debating how to handle the meeting and provide David with an unbiased evaluation when Alicia called and announced that Galen Briscoe had arrived. Quickly, I slid his file back into my bag, smoothed my dress, and walked to the office door.

I opened it, ready to greet my first client of the day, and my eyes met his. They were the color of the deepest, darkest sand and alive with something caught between humor and self–satisfaction. My heart skipped a beat and then kicked hard in my chest.

It was the man from the bar Friday night.

Chapter Thirteen

"Doctor Morgan?"

Galen's voice soothed me into a strange calmness that intrigued and scared me. I nodded because I couldn't find my voice.

"I am Galen Briscoe," he said.

He held out his hand and I took it, unprepared for the heat that surged between us, and the images came hard and fast— sweaty, intertwined bodies, his hungry mouth on mine, and a desire so desperate, so insatiable, it devoured everything we were.

I tugged out of Galen's grip, breathless and overheated and unhinged. I stared back at him and swore I could see the two of us in the depths of his sand–colored eyes. With a pounding heart, I headed for the window. I needed space and time to think, not to mention a good dose of cool, calming air.

"Take a seat," I said, unable to restrain the huskiness in my voice. Whether he took the seat or not didn't matter. In fact, I didn't even care that he may have considered my immediate disregard of him as rude, and when I opened the window and felt the fresh summer breeze rush in, it did little to temper my overheated body and the fine sheen of sweat that covered it.

"Doctor Taletta Morgan," he said, reading my diplomas from the other side of the room. "Unusual name."

Once again his voice blanketed me in a calm that eased my

alarm as quickly as his touch ignited it. It was deep and refined with a hint of an accent thrown in, and I would have asked him to continue talking just so I could keep taking pleasure in it. I closed my eyes, determined to fight the startling and primal effect he had on me, and didn't face him until the restlessness in my body subsided.

"Taletta is a derivative of Taletha," he said, peering over at me. "Did you know that?"

I shook my head, still unable to find my voice while some baser part of me took pleasure in his, wanting more. "No," I said after clearing my throat. "I didn't."

He shoved his hands in his pockets and continued browsing around my office as if it were his own. I tracked his lean body and long legs, and the form–fitting silk T–shirt and black slacks that accentuated it. Understatedly wealthy. Supremely self–confident. And an unexpected enigma to me.

"It's a biblical name," he went on. "Taletha is Aramaic for *little girl* and is taken from the phrase *taletha cumi*, meaning *little girl arise*. Jesus spoke the phrase to bring a little girl back to life."

I had the vague sense his explanation was as much a description of facts as it was an indirect question to me, but I felt at a loss as to how I should respond. The cadence and rhythm in his speech had an intoxicating effect, and on shaky legs I made my way to my armchair and sat down.

"Do you study the bible?" I asked, feeling beads of sweat form on my lower back and upper lip again.

"No." He smiled, and it was genuine and almost as alluring as his voice. "I have been very well educated, although I think you probably already knew that."

I tried focusing on the reason Galen was here in the first place and the job I had to do, but his knowing grin widened and my heart stumbled over itself once more.

"There is no need to be surprised, Doctor Morgan. I am sure you have done your research on me just as I have done on you."

He looked at me as if he saw right through me, as if he knew something about me that no one else ever could. As I watched him settle into the sofa, shifting and moving with ease, I knew this to be true. In some deep, dark place, I knew this man. Knew what moved him to passion along with what pleasured and pained him.

But I didn't know how or why.

"Do we know each other from somewhere?" I asked. "You seem so very familiar."

His eyes narrowed but he didn't answer right away. "I saw you at the bar the other night."

"No, I don't mean that. I meant do we know each other from somewhere else?"

Again, he took his time in responding. "Perhaps."

Some part of me knew he was lying.

I did my best to shrug off my fascination and pressed on. "Your educational background is exceptional," I said. "Your military and work experience is equally extraordinary. I'd like to talk more about that."

Galen leaned forward and rested his hands on his knees. "Have I come at a bad time, Doctor Morgan? You seem distracted."

I planted on a confident smile. "I'm fine."

He considered me a few moments longer. "I feel

uncomfortable about this, too," he said, settling back into the sofa. "This is the first time in my career that I've ever had to complete a secondary evaluation for a new position. And knowing that you might have power to sway the decision about me doesn't make me feel particularly confident about the process." He lowered his voice to a conspiratorial whisper. "I feel like I must be on my best behavior or be forced to face uncertain consequences."

Those last words swept over me like a lover's caress, pleasurable and full of promise, and I squeezed the armrests to steady myself. "Should I expect something else from you?" I asked.

"No. I'm simply not convinced that you will be unbiased. You are, after all," he added, "Bellotti's woman."

The inflection in Galen's voice changed and now carried a hint of jealousy that I found odd. Yet it was there, and on some level I felt compelled to soothe it.

"I assure you, Galen, that I can separate my personal life from my professional one."

He said nothing and the corners of his mouth tipped up into a subtle but evocative grin. An emotion I didn't want to identify rushed over me.

"Well, then," I said. "Let's move on, shall we? How do you enjoy working for PROs?"

"I love the work. Love the physical challenge, too."

I grabbed a notepad and pen from the end table and jotted down some notes. "What do you do for them now? What's your current job spec?"

"I'm a sniper."

I paused, feeling Galen's gaze settle on me as I stopped

writing. I'd never met someone who openly admitted they killed for a living, and I wondered if that piece of information had been excluded from his file on purpose.

"I've been doing this for nearly the entire eight years I've worked for PROs," Galen added.

"Have you ever had the desire to do something else?"

"No. My job is most rewarding. There's something to be said for taking down an authority that is not fit to be in power."

I looked up, curious about what that meant. "And how do you determine who should have power and who shouldn't?"

Galen paused. "Perhaps I didn't explain myself well. My job is not to judge, Doctor Morgan, but to do what is in the best interests of the client who hired us. There are occasions when we seize power, but that's rare. Mostly we help transition governments or regimes to a more stable leadership. Or overthrow factions that prey on the less fortunate."

They were the same politically correct words David used to describe his job to strangers, too. Words that, I knew, told only a very small part of a much bigger truth. Still, I was able to recognize that Galen had a strong moral code as well as a hearty dose of ego and superiority complex mixed in—common characteristics among the PROs professionals I'd met through David over the years. It came as no surprise that Galen had them, too.

"And what do you dislike about the work?" I asked.

"Nothing."

I didn't believe him and decided to change tactics to get a better sense of what motivated him. "What challenges do you face in your work?"

"Long periods of time away from home."

I suppressed a smile. It was David's biggest complaint, too. "Anything else?"

"No."

He was still holding back. "What about the people you work with? What can you tell me about them and your relationship with them?"

"They are strong–willed men and women. I really enjoy serving with them."

"How would you describe your relationship with your colleagues?"

"Professional." He cocked his head, curious. "You seem disappointed. Is this a problem?"

I shook my head. "No. It's just that some people enjoy spending some of their free time with co–workers to establish or strengthen friendships. At a happy hour, for example. Or at picnics or dinners."

"I don't associate those activities with work."

Interesting. "According to your records, you applied to David Bellotti's team three times before this one, and each time you were denied that application. Why?"

Had I blinked I would have missed the brief emotion that passed over Galen's face. At first I thought it was anger and then realized it was disgust. His eyes hardened to near black, giving me a glimmer of the darker, lethal side of him that had probably earned him his accolades. And that might have earned David's mistrust as well.

"Why do you think you've been rejected to join David Bellotti's team so often?"

"Let me make something clear," Galen said, leaning close enough so that one of his legs pressed against mine. "I have only the utmost respect for Bellotti. He is the best at what he does at PROs and I wouldn't be here if it was not for him."

I pulled back, trying to ignore the body heat radiating between us. "Are you saying that David Bellotti was not responsible for your rejected applications?"

His eyes searched mine, intent on finding something or maybe even seeing something in particular, but when he realized what he wanted wasn't there he pulled away. "I cannot answer your question, Doctor Morgan. Maybe you should ask Bellotti instead."

I decided that I would.

The clock showed that we had a few minutes left but I wasn't sure how to best use the rest of our time. Galen's mood had morphed into something calculating and isolated, and I felt cut off from him in a way I couldn't explain.

I also knew I didn't like it.

Galen stood and took a few steps toward the door. "I believe our time is nearly over," he said. "I think that I should go."

"We still have five more minutes."

"Doctor Morgan, do you really believe you will accomplish what you need in only a few more minutes?"

It was a challenge and an invitation I'd already considered, and I accepted both. "I'd like to arrange for another two or three sessions, if you're agreeable," I said, knowing the news wouldn't go over well with David. He would be expecting a full report and probably within the next couple of days.

"I would like that very much," Galen said, and his rich, melodious voice reached out and touched me like a lover's skilled hand. Any previous discomfort I felt was long forgotten. I only knew I wanted to hear him speak again. "Should I make the appointments with you?"

"See Alicia at the front desk," I said, escorting him to the door. "She'll handle everything."

"Thank you, Doctor Morgan. I appreciate your courtesy and your time." He took one of my hands and held it in both of his. His touch was warm and firm. And very, very familiar.

I remembered standing with him in brilliant afternoon light that reflected off a limestone–pillared courtyard. In the distance, birds with bright red tails flew overhead, canvassing the river for their next meal.

I took a step in retreat, angry that my jeweled, leather sandal had broken.

"You are worried we will be seen together," he had said, bending over to remove the sandal from my foot to fix it.

I pulled away from him and took another step in retreat. "Please stop that."

He straightened, looking genuinely confused. "Stop what?"

"Your voice," I said. "It affects me."

"Is that a bad thing?"

I looked at the red–tailed birds, hoping they could help me find a better answer. "Yes."

"Why?"

"Because I belong to another man."

"I can change that if I wanted."

I opened my mouth, ready to disagree, but once again his voice wrapped me in a delectable sweat that I felt powerless to ignore, and the fire inside me ignited into something more potent.

I offered an abrupt goodbye and as I walked down the other side of the hill, I felt the pull of him at my back. The sensation stayed with me with each step I took, and as I descended the hill only one thought filled my mind.

I needed to keep my distance from that man.

I felt warm soft lips on the back of my hand and I stared in wonder at the top of Galen's bent head. His fingers slid from my hand but the feel of his lips remained, and as I watched him turn away and walk down the hall to the front desk, I knew one thing for certain. Galen was the man from my memory. I saw it in his eyes, heard it in his voice, felt it in his touch. And I had a strong feeling that he knew it, too.

I realized that keeping contact with Galen, even on just a professional level, was going to be dangerous. I also realized that I would have to tell David.

And I was dreading it.

Chapter Fourteen

I barreled through the garage door and into the kitchen, dropped my handbag on the counter, and headed straight for the wine rack. I rummaged through a drawer for the corkscrew, found a wine glass, opened a bottle of Merlot, and poured without any consideration for neatness or desire to let the wine breathe.

David stood by the stove, stirring something in a deep pan, watching me while Saving Abel filtered through the speakers in the background. He said nothing, probably because he'd been able to judge my mood, and I was grateful for it. I wasn't ready to talk to him about Galen yet, and the only way I'd get there was if I took the edge off first.

I took a few sips, trying to relieve the stress and relax my mind because I'd been unable to concentrate on anyone other than Galen for the entire day. He'd taken over my psyche to the point of compulsion, and I knew I'd done my clients a disservice because I didn't give them my full attention. I'd been professional enough for their sessions, but only barely.

I gritted my teeth and squeezed my eyes shut, trying to erase the mental image of Galen, of *us*, and couldn't do it. The memories kept coming at me, over and over again, and I was nearly out of my mind when I decided dainty sips weren't doing the trick. I downed the rest of the glass in three gulps while David kept watching.

He dropped a large spoon on the counter, wiped his hands on a towel and turned his full attention on me. "What happened?"

"Not now, David."

I poured a second glass of wine and dove into that one, too.

David had the good sense not to pursue the discussion further but I knew the courtesy wouldn't last forever. Even people who were psychologically strongest couldn't fight curiosity's temptation forever.

A large pan rattled on the stove and started to smoke, and by the time David realized what was happening, dinner had turned charred and black. With a curse, he grabbed the pan, shut off the gas and stood by the burner, assessing the damage.

"Sorry dinner got ruined," I said, walking toward the slider. "We can clean it up together later on." Though whatever he'd been making—and it looked like spiced sausage, tomatoes and peppers—had been a heavy loss. David was the best cook I knew.

Outside, I settled into a chaise lounge and stared up at the stars. It was an unusually bright night, free of clouds and the pollution that normally dulled what was now a brilliant, diamond–dotted sky.

The slider opened and closed, and David walked over and joined me. "Just answer me one question and I'll let this go," he said, taking the chaise next to mine. "Did anything happen today that I should know about? Anything that endangered your life?"

"No," I said, and David nodded, satisfied with the answer.

He poured a glass of wine for himself and showed me the

half–empty bottle as well as a second he'd brought along as backup, an implicit promise that both were ready for when I wanted more. We sat in silence, drinking and watching the heavens, and I let myself be carried away by the constellations and planets that seemed so close and yet so far away. I thought about their names and how they may have gotten them, and the rituals our ancestors had used to appease them in their beliefs that they were gods. By the time the second bottle was nearly empty almost two hours later, my anxiety had been dulled enough for me to talk.

"David?" I turned my head and saw him stretched out on the chaise with his hands clasped behind his head and his eyes closed. "Are you asleep?"

"Nope." His eyes opened and he fixed them firmly on mine, and even in the darkness their green color appeared unnaturally bright. They were the one physical feature of David's that always took my breath away, but even more so now because of how they reflected the bright moon and stars.

"I need to talk to you about something."

He didn't move but I knew that I had his attention because his face showed wariness, and for good reason. I never prefaced any conversation unless it was going to be a difficult one.

"Okay," he said.

I sat up and faced him. "I want to tell you about what happened today, but I need two things from you first."

His eyes narrowed, and then he adjusted his chaise so that he could sit upright, too. "Okay."

"First," I said, "I need you to have an open mind."

He stilled as if he'd been held in suspended animation, and

for a moment I wondered if he had stopped breathing. "Okay."

It was the same response for the third time and I wondered if I was getting through. "I'm serious, David."

He gave me a long look. "So am I."

"Okay. Well, that's good." I thought about how to ask the second request without setting him off but when I realized that there was no delicate way around it, I decided to jump right into it. "The other thing is this. In order for me to be able to explain what happened, I'll need Paul here to do it. I need the three of us together."

David pushed out of the chair and started collecting the bottles and glasses, ignoring my request and letting me know I shouldn't have even bothered to try. I didn't like being shoved aside in that way and I was going to let him know it.

"You have to let go of this sometime." The two glasses clinked sharply in his hands and I cringed, worried they would break under his reckless care. "It's not healthy for you or for us to carry emotional baggage that doesn't have anything to do with where we are now as a couple."

"This isn't emotional baggage," he snapped, angry now and making sure I knew it. "You cheated on me with this man, and you want to invite him into our home? Not going to happen, Lottie." He walked toward the slider, making it clear that the conversation was done.

I got up and followed. He wasn't going to run away, damn it. Not this time. "We were separated when that happened. It wasn't cheating."

"Really?" He turned on me and what stared back in that darkened yard made me pause and then shudder. This was the side of David that I never saw; the side that was dangerous and deadly and that did things I didn't want to know about. "I don't recall ever breaking it off with you at that time. We never said the words and we never made that decision."

"But we weren't together either," I reminded him. "For months and months things weren't going well for us. And for a long time we didn't even see each other."

David closed the distance between us, all fired up and ready to fight. "So that means that if we hit a bad spot in our relationship right now, I can go out and sleep with whoever I want?"

I staggered back, thrown off balance by the verbal blow. "Things are different now," I said. "We've grown stronger. We're not the same couple we were back then."

But even as I reasoned with him, I knew I wasn't getting through. As much as Paul had become a dear friend of mine over time, he would remain the one unresolved issue between David and me. And judging by the look on David's face, I had a feeling it would always stay that way.

"You have to believe me, David. I need this. I need the three of us together because—"

"Find another psychiatrist. Use the one from PROs that I use. But not Paul. It's not going to happen." He turned and went for the door.

"This isn't fair," I said. "You're forcing me into a situation you don't want me to be in and that you're not prepared to handle."

My warning stopped David mid–stride.

"Don't push me into making a decision that could ruin us, David. This isn't about ego or who's right or who's wrong. This is about us." I paused. "And my mental health."

He turned only his head, showing me a hardened, shadowed profile. And in that short moment, where nothing moved and time seemed to stand still, I realized I might have my only chance of finding a compromise.

"Please, David. Please do this for me." My request sounded desperate even to me, and I realized I'd started to cry. "I couldn't stand losing you again and you have to know that I wouldn't do anything to risk that. But you have to work with me here. Paul can help me find answers that no one else can. You have to believe me. I wouldn't ask otherwise."

For a long while we both stood in silence, and eventually David's tense and rigid posture softened. After what felt like an eternity, he put the bottles and glasses on the patio, pulled his cell phone from his jeans pocket and handed it over to me.

"Call Paul and have him come over tonight."

He took the glassware and went inside without another word.

Chapter Fifteen

David and I didn't speak while we waited for Paul and I knew why. David needed space and I was more than willing to give it to him. In my mind, he'd taken a huge emotional step with Paul, but I didn't view it as his complete acceptance of the man either. It was just David's way of trying to do the right thing.

When the doorbell rang, David ushered Paul inside while I remained on the couch and out of the way. I had no doubt that the alpha male in David would strike if given even the smallest chance, but I also had no doubt that Paul would fight back. I just didn't want to get in the middle if it happened.

Both men entered the den in silence, and Paul remained standing just inside the room as David sat down beside me. I watched Paul, feeling a little sorry for him. Not only had I dragged him to my house at almost eleven at night, I'd drawn him into a potentially volatile situation that would once again remind him that he wasn't the man I'd ultimately chosen.

I smiled at him, more than grateful for what he'd done now and in the past. "Thank you for coming here," I said. "I know it's very late."

Paul's gaze volleyed between David and me. He was on alert and, it seemed, figuring the quickest route out of the house if he needed it. "It's okay. It sounded important."

His hesitation hummed through me. "It's definitely important and you're the only person who can help."

Paul's eyes shifted to David again, gauging his mood and, like me, probably wondering what was lurking behind his quiet demeanor. "What happened?" he asked.

"You remember the conversation you and I had about memories?"

Paul nodded.

"I had another one today that I need to talk about."

"What memories?" David asked.

"I'll explain in a minute," I told him.

Paul folded his arms over his chest and didn't budge from the doorway. Though he stood motionless, I could see the strain of tension in his body. He was annoyed that I didn't tell him that David was home, and he also now knew that I had kept the information from him on purpose. We both knew he wouldn't have come otherwise.

I gestured to the leather chairs but Paul didn't sit.

"I met with a new client this morning and I think I know him from somewhere."

"Galen?" David asked.

I nodded.

"Conflict of interest?" Paul asked.

"I'm not sure."

"How do you know him?" David asked.

I hesitated because the explanation wasn't going to be easy. "It's a long story."

Paul tilted his head in a gesture I knew well. He'd already made the connection. "Galen is a piece of the memories you told me about."

"Exactly."

"What memories?" David repeated.

When I turned to David, I carefully considered my words. I didn't want to patronize him but I didn't want him to misunderstand either.

"These episodes I've been having over the past few days aren't episodes at all, David. They're memories and—"

"How many have you had, Lottie?"

"Several."

"And you didn't tell me?"

"I didn't know how to explain what I couldn't figure out for myself. I needed the time to understand and now I realize that Galen is a key."

"How can you know Galen or have a memory of him but not remember who he was when you studied his file?"

I shifted on the sofa, uncomfortable, because he'd verbalized a question that nagged at me all day. "That's why I asked Paul here. Galen's a trigger and an integral part of these memories. I know him, or knew him, but I can't figure out how."

"A repressed memory?" Paul asked.

"It doesn't feel like one." I sorted through the dozens of thoughts and images I'd already associated with Galen, but none of them came together in any sort of coherent way. "When I met Galen this morning, we shook hands and when we made contact, I had a very vivid, very strong memory. The strongest out of any of them."

"Has Galen been a part of all of the memories?"

"It doesn't seem like it but I'm not completely sure. I didn't realize it at first because I couldn't place the face until today. But I still can't place the time." I shrugged. "I can only say that the memories feel old."

"How old?"

I sifted through the images again, trying to peg down at least one that could give me a clue but I came up empty. "I don't know. I can't see them clearly. I see snippets but nothing long enough to give me the information I need."

"But you said today's memory was very vivid. What was different about that one that made it more clear to you?"

"It wasn't that it was clear, Paul. It was more the feelings and sensations that came alive for me that had an impact. And the emotions lingered for a long time after." Too long, in fact.

"What kind of feelings did you experience?"

I glanced at David, knowing he wouldn't like the answer. "Sexual."

David's jaw locked. "You've slept with Galen."

"No. Well, yes, but no."

"Which is it? Yes or no?"

"David, I understand that this may make you feel upset—"

"This isn't about being upset," he shot back, but his tone betrayed him. David wasn't just upset. He was bordering on infuriated. "This is important, Lottie. Galen is in line to join my team and you were going to evaluate him today. Now, tonight, I learn that you not only know him but that you've slept with him."

"Whatever past Galen and I had shouldn't impact his role on your team."

"No?"

"No."

"Are these details in your report?"

I swallowed over a dry throat. I'd promised David a complete evaluation and I couldn't give it to him. Not right away, anyway. "I didn't complete Galen's evaluation because a half hour wasn't enough time to do what I needed to do. I tried to make it work because you wanted a report quickly, but I need to meet with him again to do this properly."

"I see."

"You can move ahead without my input," I reminded him. "You already have the go–ahead from PROs. You don't need me or my evaluation on this one."

"That's not the point and you know it, Lottie."

"That's right. I *do* know it. And I also know that I'm going to sort this out with or without you and if you want to be of any help, you'll find that open mind you promised me earlier."

David's eyes fired with impatience but I'd called his bluff and we both knew that he had only two choices. Neither was perfect but one was clearly worse than the other. And it became obvious that David realized that very quickly too, because he let out a long sigh that sounded more from resignation than a need to expel pent–up, restrained hot air.

"Look," I said, recognizing the subtle shift in David's mood. "I know this isn't what you want to hear, and I also know that my professional thoughts about Galen are important to you and your decision, but there's something else going on that's much bigger than what we anticipated."

David rubbed his hands over his face but it did little to hide the fatigue that shadowed his eyes and the edginess that threatened to drive us into an argument that might not be settled for days.

"I'm working very hard here," he said, dropping his hands to his lap.

"I know."

He let out a long breath, still troubled. "I still don't understand how you could have slept with Galen and not remember who he is."

"It's not what you think. I remember all the men I've slept with." I stopped, quickly catching my slip–up. "You remember who you've been with, don't you? Not necessarily all the details, or maybe even all the names." One side of David's mouth quirked with a grin. "But you remember something, right?"

"I remember."

"That's my point. I look at Galen and see these memories but I don't know why I have them."

Paul leaned in. "I still think this is a repressed memory coming to surface. It's a very logical and rational explanation. Perhaps you had an experience with Galen that you didn't want to remember because it was distressing to you."

"Whatever Galen and I had was very passionate and intense. It doesn't seem like something I would repress." Which made me wonder how I could even forget it to begin with. Galen was not a forgettable man.

"That still doesn't mean it's not a false memory," Paul said. "Or that your memory is accurate."

"True, but what I'm remembering is real, Paul. I know it is because I can feel it. This isn't something I made up in my head as a substitute for an inadequacy or a shortcoming."

"And feelings have also been known to be inexact. They're not always a measure of reality."

I stilled, unsure of the meaning behind his words and if they belonged in this particular conversation.

"They may be inexact, Paul, but that doesn't make them

any less real."

"Real feelings can be very different than reality," he said. "They're not completely indicative of truth."

"But they *are* a pathway."

"If one is honest enough to find that path."

"Are we all still talking about the same thing?" David asked. "Or have you moved onto a conversation I don't know about?"

Paul withdrew and folded his arms over his chest again.

"I just want to find out why this is happening to me and what it means," I said. "I want to find sense in emotions and thoughts that don't have any right now."

My thoughts and feelings about Galen felt real, and yet they defied every rational, educated part of my brain. I didn't know him and yet I did. I'd never been with him, and yet my body told me otherwise. I didn't know why I felt what I felt and the more I concentrated on Galen, the more confused I became.

I felt tension tighten around my chest and press down, hard, and I was starting to have trouble finding air. I gulped in several breaths, feeling light–headed, and then the room started to sway.

"I don't feel very good," I said, sliding down onto a pillow and pulling my legs up onto David's lap.

The back of David's hand found my forehead. "She feels clammy."

"I'll get her a glass of water," Paul said.

I closed my eyes and heard cabinets open and shut until Paul found the glass he needed. David stroked my forehead and hushed me into calmer breathing, and when Paul returned I drank as if I hadn't had water for days.

David put the empty glass on the coffee table and Paul knelt by my side, watching. I concentrated on the feel of David's warm, sure caress and studied the ceiling, focusing on a tiny imperfection in the white paint.

"Your color's coming back," Paul said. "Feeling better?"

"I think so," I said.

"What happened?"

"Don't know."

"Do you want more water?" David asked.

I remembered the water again. And I was running now. Running and laughing after a boy named Bakari but he was too fast to follow, and he dove into the river, laughing at me as he disappeared below the surface.

"Bakari!" I screamed. "There are crocodiles!"

I skidded to a stop at the edge of the river, kicking mud up onto my sandals and legs, but I did not care. I did not know where he had gone and that scared me. I watched the water, looking for ripples or bubbles that would tell me he was fine, but nothing moved and I started to panic. What if he had drowned? What if something had happened? What if the crocodiles got to him and—?

Bakari jumped up, breaking the surface in a large spray of water, and laughed like I had never heard him laugh before.

"You are mad!" I yelled, pretending to be angry but he was laughing too hard and that made me laugh, too.

"Come on in," he called out, and he splashed me with water that felt cool and smelled like clean, crisp linen.

"We will get in trouble," I called back.

Bakari held out his arms. "So?"

I laughed even harder. He was so daring and so sure of himself, and no matter how many times he was given extra chores because of his defiance, all meant to teach him a lesson that he did not want to learn, he still did not care. Nothing ever stopped Bakari, and as I watched him dive back down into the river, I thought nothing ever would.

When he came up for air the second time, he grinned at me. "How are we to have any fun, Shemei, if we stay away from all the fun?"

"There are other ways to have fun that will not kill us," I giggled.

"Ways that are boring. What good is this life if we do not live it?"

"Do not say such things," I gasped. "We are not only about this life, Bakari, but the one after it as well."

"And I ask again," he said with outstretched arms, "what good is this life if we do not live it?"

I could not find the answer. The sun felt hot and the wind off the sands even hotter, and I would have liked nothing more than to cool off even for a little bit. But there were still crocodiles out there and one other small thing that, to me, was not so small.

"I have nothing to wear, Bakari. I have only my sheath and I did not bring a change of clothes."

"So?"

"It will get wet."

"So?" Bakari waded toward me, not caring that his own linen kilt was soaked. "That is what water does, Shemei." He swiped his hands down his arms, half to dry them and half to tease me with another spray of cool water.

"And you wonder why you are always in trouble," I said. "You cannot seem to help yourself. And I bet your mother would agree."

I looked past his shoulder and to his mother, Hebeny, who was walking toward us. Hebeny kept a steady, ceremonial gait, and one that I always admired because she truly looked like a goddess from above. Her linen sheath shimmered with threads of fine gold, while the gold bracelets, armlets and anklets she wore reflected the bright sun as if they were suns themselves. Even the gold in her braided wig sparkled and I wondered if I would ever look as beautiful as she did.

"My mother?" Bakari swung around but it was too late for him to get away. His mother grabbed his sidelock and yanked, not too hard but hard enough.

"What do you think you are doing?" she asked. "Why are you not at studies this afternoon?"

"We had a break."

"Then why are the other students in class?" She yanked harder.

"Hey!" he cried out. "That hurt!"

"Not as much as getting injured or killed on a battlefield," she scolded. "Is this the way a future general behaves?"

"No, *mawat*," Bakari said.

"Do you think that every time you get bored or hot, you can just run off and play?"

"No, *mawat*."

"Do you think that the soldiers you will eventually command will take direction from someone who does not take his role seriously?"

"No, *mawat*." Bakari looked at me and rolled his eyes. He

slid out from her grasp and stared at her, and I held my breath. I knew what he was going to say before he even said it. "Who says I want to be a general anyway?"

"Bite your tongue, Bakari!" Her hands went to her hips. "Your father is a general, and his father was a general. Every male in this family has served the royal family and its army, and so will you."

"But—"

"Get back to your studies, Bakari. Now."

Bakari scowled and I felt sad. I wanted to spend the afternoon with him. We did not have many days left together before he would leave the royal court and my life for good, and before my own future would be sealed when my brother took the throne and found me someone to marry.

"Yes, *mawat*," Bakari said. "I will return to class."

His shoulders slumped and he trudged away with a loud sigh. Hebeny headed in the other direction, back to our village and the royal court in the center of it. I watched her disappear over a small hill and into the valley in the distance, and then turned and watched the ripples in the water. It was going to be lonely here when Bakari was gone.

Mad, I kicked a pebble into the river and watched a school of fish scurry away. Maybe I had made a mistake in not swimming with him, dangerous as it could have been. But could–have–been did not always mean definitely–would–be, and I had lost out on a wonderful chance to—

Bakari came charging out of the brush, grabbed me by the arm and hurtled the both of us into the river. We flopped over each other, splashed each other, and laughed until our sides hurt, and not once did I complain about crocodiles or my wet sheath. We never did make it back to wherever we should have been that day, and we both paid the price to our parents when we returned home for Last Meal. But my punishment of having to translate ten scrolls in two days had been worth it.

The vision of glittering water and sunbaked sand disappeared, and David was looking at me, his eyes as green as the thin–leafed reeds that edged the river in my memory.

He sat down beside me and brushed my hair from my face. "Are you okay?"

I nodded. "I saw another memory."

"About Galen?" he asked.

"No," I said. "This memory was about you."

Chapter Sixteen

I was looking at David and trying to tie in the boy from my memory to the man I knew and loved now and couldn't find a connection. I'd known David since he was two and I was one, and nothing I'd seen in that vision even came close to the childhood we shared.

"This doesn't make sense," I said.

Paul squatted down in front of me. "What happened?"

I hesitated, still trying to get my own head around what I had experienced. I recounted the episode slowly as I carefully pulled at the entangled threads of my past and present, separating them in my mind as I went.

"But that wasn't my childhood," David said when I finished.

"Except for the part about you always getting into trouble?" I shook my head. "No, it wasn't."

"My mother's name isn't Hebeny. It's Rita. And who are Bakari and Shemei?"

"I don't know."

I sat up, teased by a vague and formless mental picture filled with carefree, happy emotions that hinted of another life I couldn't identify.

"Maybe we're looking at this the wrong way, Lottie," David said. "Maybe these aren't memories after all."

"That's a very strong possibility," Paul said.

"No." I pushed off the sofa, determined to find answers, and faced them. "These are memories. I'm sure of it because I can feel it in here," I said, pointing to my heart. "And I know it in here," I added, pointing to my head.

David came to me. "But that wasn't me, Lottie. I know how I grew up, and so do you, so how can these be memories if I didn't live any part of what you've just told me?"

"It wasn't a story, David."

"And that wasn't my childhood."

"But I was *there*. We both were *there*."

"Maybe you should sit down, Lottie," Paul suggested. "Get some rest."

"Neither of you understands any of this. Or me."

I strode out of the den and ran up the stairs to the spare bedroom we used as an office. David followed, and Paul came in seconds later.

"What are you doing?" David asked as I powered up the computer and launched a browser and a search engine.

"Looking."

"For what?"

"Explanations," I said. "Clarifications." Anything.

My fingers flew over the keyboard and I plugged in the names and details I remembered, then watched the search engine kick back results. None of them were helpful.

I slumped in the chair, feeling even more confused. "These are all Egyptian websites," I said. "Why do my memories link to Egyptian history and narrative?"

Paul shifted on his feet and his silence started bothering me.

"You're thinking something," I said. "What is it?"

Paul exchanged a look with David, and David nodded. "I'd like to suggest a couple of counseling sessions," Paul said. "I think they will be helpful to you right now. I have time tomorrow afternoon and I'd be more than happy to spend it with you."

"My God. You think I'm crazy. That I've lost my mind."

"Lottie—"

"It's true. Isn't it?"

When Paul didn't answer, I turned on David. "You've known me for my entire life, David. Answer me. It's the least you can do." I squeezed the armrests and held my breath, angry and irritated that I couldn't get through.

"I think," he said slowly, "that Paul's suggestion is a good one."

All the air escaped from the room and my lungs, and I tried steeling myself against a sudden and potent surge of self–doubt.

"Lottie," David said in a soft voice, "I can understand that you're feeling confused."

"Now you're patronizing me."

"No, I'm not. We can talk about this but that can only happen if you settle down."

I shoved out of the chair and started for the door and my bedroom down the hall. "You're not listening to me!"

"Lottie!"

I felt David hard on my heels, trying to stop me. I dodged his grip before he could take hold.

"Leave me alone," I said, slamming the bedroom door in his face. It was childish behavior and I didn't care. I only wanted to be taken seriously. I only wanted them to understand.

I paced the bedroom then shrugged out of my dress and threw on a yellow T–shirt and striped girlie boxers and got into bed. Every now and then, I glanced at the clock on the nightstand and watched time tick away until David came in nearly thirty minutes later.

He stripped and slid into bed next to me. "You want to talk about it?" he asked.

"No."

"I understand that you're upset," David said, rolling away, "but next time you might want to consider giving me a little more credit than you did tonight."

"Only if you can do the same," I said, and I rolled away from him, too.

Chapter Seventeen

David's side of the bed was cold and empty when the alarm went off for work the next morning. I took a quick shower, fixed my hair and makeup and slipped into a pale blue blouse, floral skirt and sandals. When I entered the kitchen, David greeted me with a guarded look.

He pointed to the fresh, dark brew in the coffee maker. "High test, if you need it. And if you're in the mood, I also picked up fresh bagels after my run this morning."

I noticed that David was freshly shaven and had traded his running gear for a black tee and a pair of jeans. I spied the brown bag on the counter, peeked inside, grabbed a sesame bagel and took a few bites. It was still warm and smelled like a small slice of heaven. David's tablet was on the kitchen table, open to the latest news. I picked it up and browsed through it.

David kept watching me. "I want to talk," he said.

I put down the tablet.

He put down his coffee. "What got into you last night?"

"Neither of you believed me and, quite frankly, I got angry. I deserve better."

"That wasn't angry. That was…" He stopped, thought for a few moments, and shook his head. "You were acting weird, Lottie. You know it as well as I do."

We both sat at the table, neither looking at the other, and the psychologist in me imagined what another psychologist would have construed from our body language. We may have only sat three feet apart from each other, but it could just as easily have been three hundred.

David downed what was left in his mug, set it on the table, and focused all his energy on me. "Regardless of what's right or wrong or real, you didn't behave like yourself last night. I have no idea where the behavior came from, but it was childish and rude and I didn't deserve it."

"I wanted to be heard and understood," I said. "And that wasn't happening."

"What did you expect, Lottie? The story you told made no sense because that's just what it sounded like. A story."

"It's a memory. I don't know how else to get this through to you."

"And if the situation was reversed and it was me telling you all of this, what would you be thinking?"

I'd thought of that before and didn't have an answer.

"I tried to be patient and listen, Lottie. I tried working with you and understanding what you're going through. And the ironic part is, just when I agreed that Paul should come here and help, you had a meltdown and slammed a door in my face. I'm not kidding when I say that I came this close to sleeping in the spare bedroom last night.

"You've been reminding me lately about how far we've come as a couple, but last night I felt like we were children all over again. So just how far do you want me to go? How much do you want me to take without saying a word, despite the fact that we've promised each other over and over again to be honest with each other? Because after last night, I'm not so sure what the hell is going on and I'm not sure how much patience I have left. I gave it everything I had and I still got treated like crap."

In my heart I knew he was right and yet I still felt like he didn't understand, and nothing seemed to make a difference no matter how hard I tried. David didn't believe me. No one, it seemed, believed me, and I desperately wanted to change that.

I checked my watch and used the time as an excuse to end the conversation. "I have to go to work."

David grabbed my hand. "We're not going to ignore this. This isn't going to disappear just because you have to go to work."

"I know." Of course, I knew.

But how I desperately wanted to make him see. And maybe I was asking for too much. Maybe I was pushing the limits of a man who viewed life so differently from me that he couldn't believe what couldn't so easily be believed.

I disengaged from David, recognizing that he wasn't wired that way and never would be. And, for the first time in years, it felt disappointing.

I grabbed my bag and keys and David walked me to the garage. Like always, he watched me pull out of the driveway but this time we didn't kiss each other goodbye. By the time I pulled into Amrose's parking lot, my head was full of David and everything unresolved between us and I was grateful for the steady flow of clients on my calendar. Anything that would help me keep him off my mind.

By the time noon rolled around and I had seen three clients, I felt hungry and ready for a break. While I was debating what to eat and from where, Alicia called from the front desk.

"Mrs. Reynolds is here to see you," she said.

"Are you sure?" I checked my cell phone, thinking that someone slotted her into my calendar and forgot to tell me. But she wasn't there.

Alicia responded with silence. She never made a mistake with clients or appointments, and she didn't make one this time either. "Shall I send her in?" she asked.

I sank in my chair, wondering why Mrs. Reynolds changed her mind about meeting with me now. "Yes, please."

A minute later, Mrs. Reynolds appeared at the doorframe and took a few steps inside. Her long blonde hair was pulled into a tight knot, her green Gucci dress looked brand new, and the small smile on her face seemed gentle and apologetic.

"Is this a good time?" she asked.

"Certainly." I gestured to the sofa and made my way to meet her there.

"No, thank you," she said. "I won't be long." She took a few more tentative steps inside. "I thought about our conversation the other day and I would like to arrange some sessions with you."

"I'd be more than happy to arrange counseling with you, Mrs. Reynolds."

"Do you have something available right away?"

"You can check with Alicia at the reception desk. She handles all of my appointments."

Mrs. Reynolds seemed pleased with the suggestion. "I will do that. Thank you."

She lingered in the doorway.

"Is there something else you want to talk about?" I asked.

"No." Then she turned and left, the remnants of her Chanel

perfume trailing behind her.

The scent intensified, then changed, and I no longer smelled Chanel but something deeper. More powerful. My servant was at my side, rubbing myrrh and sweet wine on my arms and legs. She asked me if I enjoyed the new oils. I told her that I did.

Kesi.

The woman's name surfaced from my unconscious mind and I knew that the voice I heard, the hands I felt on my body, belonged to her.

The memory disappeared and I hurried down the hall to Alicia, catching her in the middle of a phone call.

"Did Mrs. Reynolds make any appointments with you?" I asked.

Alicia disconnected the call and gave me a blank look. "Appointments for what?"

"She said she wanted to arrange therapy. Didn't she stop by to see you?"

"I was at the printer for a few minutes and wasn't watching the reception area," Alicia said. "If she came back here, she definitely didn't wait for me."

I blew out a sigh, knowing I shouldn't have been surprised but feeling it all the same. I spun around, headed down the hall, found Paul's open door and strode inside. Paul looked up from his computer when I walked in.

"Something's very wrong, Paul."

And I felt pretty certain that it was with me.

Chapter Eighteen

Paul met me at the office door and escorted me to a chair. "You look white as a ghost," he said, taking a seat beside me. "Are you okay?"

"I don't know. I don't understand what's happening."

My thoughts were racing too fast for me to make sense of them. Mrs. Reynolds was exhibiting erratic behavior and, if I wanted to be truthful, I felt pretty sure I was starting to do it, too.

"Logan's mother wants to start therapy with me," I said. "At least she said that she did, but she left without making any appointments." I looked to Paul for answers. "I'm trying to understand why she's behaving this way, but nothing's adding up. It feels like she's playing games with me, Paul. I realize that sounds a bit like paranoia, but I'm sensing that something else is going on with her."

"Maybe you misunderstood her."

"I didn't misunderstand anything. What she said, and how she said it, couldn't have been more clear."

"You haven't been well, Lottie. And, given what you've been experiencing lately, it's entirely possible that this is a gross misinterpretation of reality."

Paul reached for me but I stood up before he could make contact. I started walking the small office, trying to work out the details as I paced. "She's manipulating me and telling me lies, which, I realize, isn't anything new for a client to do."

Paul patted the seat I'd vacated moments before. But I wasn't in the mood to sit. Not yet. "You have to remember that you're taking input from someone you hardly know, Lottie, and under circumstances that are trying, at the very least."

"I know."

"You don't sound like you believe it." Paul came to me and fixed me with sobering, brown eyes. "You're experiencing gaps of conscious memory and creating alternative realities, but it's not like this can't be resolved."

"I know that, too."

"I hear a but in there somewhere."

"I'm worried, Paul. If this gets out, if what I've been experiencing is discovered by the rest of the Amrose staff, or worse Director Hanley, I could be put on medical leave or be suspended. I can't have that happen. I don't *want* it to happen."

"That's why you have me, right? I can provide the guidance and therapy you need and Hanley will never need to know."

"Really?"

Because we both knew that we could hide one or two conversations, maybe even three, but not long-term therapy. I blew out a breath, hoping it wouldn't come to that, brushed the hair off my face and sat down again.

"These memories are genuine," I said, wanting desperately for Paul to see what I had seen and experience what I had experienced. "They're not episodic or false. They are real images of things that actually happened."

Paul sat down, reached over and took my hands in his. "Look at me, Lottie. I'm not here to argue with you, and if I were truly worried about you, we'd be talking about specific mental disorders and related medication and therapies. But we're not doing that."

And I felt grateful for it.

"Still," he added, "we both know something is happening to you and I want to help you as much as you want to be helped. And you know that's not going to work if you keep pushing back. You can't do this alone. It's not healthy or productive."

I remembered saying similar words to Deborah just before she committed suicide.

Paul pressed his lips together and studied me from a new perspective. "How are things at work lately?"

I paused. "Is this the psychiatrist talking or the friend?"

He said nothing and waited for an answer.

"Fine. Work is fine."

"You have a heavier workload lately? Too many challenging clients all at once? Too many long hours?"

"No," I said. "I'm not stressed at work. And I'm certainly not transferring any personal issues onto my professional life, if that's what you mean."

"That wasn't what I asked," he said, and he tilted his head in that familiar way of his, making it clear that he was onto something else. "Is there a problem with your personal life?"

"Oh, come on, Paul. You of all people know that psychiatrists shouldn't read minds."

His expression flashed with brief annoyance before settling back into cool, professional mode. "Answer me, Lottie."

I didn't like his line of thinking and I definitely didn't like the way he'd asked the question. It sounded much too subtle and far too personal.

"How are things with David?" he asked. "Is your relationship still satisfying?"

Now I was on the defensive. "Of course it is."

"That's not the impression I got last night."

"Last night was not an overall indicator of whether or not our relationship is still satisfying. Occasional tension between couples is normal, Paul."

"I agree, but I was there when you railed on David and I had a suspicion that something else may have been fueling it. Something other than the episode you had. That's all, and that's the only reason I asked. You've been dealing with a lot, maybe too much, and I'm trying to help you recognize the emotional and mental consequences of what you've been facing."

He was right, of course, and I took the time to gather my thoughts. "Mostly I was angry that David didn't believe me last night, and I reacted."

"You can't blame him for that, Lottie. Even I know a few details about David, including some things about his childhood. Not a lot, but enough to know that it didn't match what you were telling us."

"It wasn't only that," I admitted. "After the memory, I remembered how David used to pick fights with me when we were kids, just because he could." Although now, I understood those fights for what they were—a boy's way of trying to get a girl's attention in an indirect, juvenile way. "I think those emotions flared up after the memory, and all I wanted to do was fight with him all over again. It was stupid and it was defensive, but it was how I felt."

"And perhaps that residual emotion colored some of what you're experiencing now?"

"Perhaps."

Paul leaned in closer, his tone and expression becoming more serious. "You're facing an emotional crossroads, Lottie, and it's not just with you."

"You mean David."

"Yes. Your relationship is changing and I don't think you're prepared for that change."

No, I wasn't. And that bothered me.

Paul's hand came up, like he was thinking about caressing my hair the way he used to, then he reconsidered and folded his hand over the other.

"For what it's worth," he said, "I really do believe that there may be, at this stage, a link between your episodes and your personal life."

"Again, you mean David."

Paul nodded. "It's a strong possibility but we'd need to talk about this more. And I have a sense that what's been happening with Mrs. Reynolds is also feeding your anxiety."

I got up again and moved to his desk, overwhelmed by his presence and all the open–ended, unanswered possibilities. "But that still doesn't answer how this all correlates with Logan."

"I don't know if it does but I'd like to help you find out."

As I thought about it more, I realized it was probably the best decision. "I'd like that."

"Good." Paul went to his desk and checked his computer. "I have this afternoon open, and a few spots here and there for the rest of the week."

"I'd rather do this at my house," I said. "Starting this afternoon, if possible. I don't have any more appointments for the rest of the day."

Paul looked ready to object but I cut him off.

"This isn't something I feel comfortable doing at Amrose," I explained. "Too many eyes and too many ears. All of them ready to psychoanalyze."

And maybe put me on temporary leave.

Paul shifted on his feet, unsure. I knew he was thinking about David and if he'd be there when he met, but he never voiced the question. He pulled a set of keys from his drawer instead.

"I'm going to take a bio break," he said. "I'll meet you in the parking lot and then we can go."

I went to my office, grabbed my handbag and keys, and headed to the parking lot and my Jeep, moving swiftly to avoid the day's crushing heat.

I turned over the engine and sat, waiting in the air conditioning. I thought about what Paul had said, that maybe my emotional stress with David was exacerbating what I was experiencing now, maybe even causing it. It made sense. The mind used a number of defensive mechanisms to cope with problems and trauma.

As I scanned the forest of large oaks and scrubby pines that lined the parking lot, I thought more about my relationship with David. I didn't like that Paul could see the tension between us so easily, but then again that's what friends did. Saw the things you didn't or couldn't, and then helped you through it.

Only Paul wasn't just a friend.

I sighed and stared out into the trees, trying to find answers. Something moved between a cluster of oaks directly in front of my Jeep. Or rather, someone. I leaned forward, trying to get a better look.

It was a woman with blonde hair.

"Mrs. Reynolds?" I said out loud, but only because I wasn't sure it was her.

She was walking through the trees, her back toward me, and moving deeper into a thicket. I lost sight of her for a moment until she reappeared in a stream of sunlight that cut through the foliage, her blonde hair now the dark braided swathe that I'd seen on the servant in my memories.

I grabbed my bag, opened the door and stepped out into the heat, ready to give chase. Whoever had been there was gone.

If someone had been there at all.

My cell buzzed with a text message. I stood in the baking sun, dug out the phone from my bag and read the display.

You trust too easily.

A shuddering chill swept over me when I realized there was no name or caller ID. I fumbled with the small keys as I typed, determined to find out who'd sent the message.

Who are you?

I waited for a reply but nothing happened. I scanned the parking lot looking for the mysterious woman again, or anything else that seemed out of place, but came up empty.

I tried the same text again. *Who are you???*

Several seconds ticked by.

You shouldn't sit alone in a parking lot. You never know

who is watching. Or why.

Chapter Nineteen

Someone tapped my shoulder and I jumped.

My hand flew to my heart, pounding like a caged animal inside my chest, while Paul stood at my side.

"Ready to go?" he asked. His expression turned grim when he saw the obvious terror on my face. "What happened?"

I shoved the cell phone at him but didn't speak. Every word, every breath, stayed lodged inside my throat.

"Who sent this?" he asked.

"I don't know." But I knew how to find out. "I have to go," I said, stealing the phone from him, getting into the Jeep and throwing it into reverse, and I sped off letting Paul decide whether or not to follow and hoping I didn't get pulled over for speeding along the way.

When I got home, I revved the Jeep up the driveway and into the garage, jumped out and raced through the laundry room and the kitchen.

"David?" I did a three–sixty but didn't find him. "David!" I yelled, running into the foyer. "Are you home?"

No one answered.

"David!" I checked the den and the backyard sliders and barreled right into his hard–muscled chest. The impact propelled me backward, and David grabbed me before I hit the floor.

"What's going on?" he asked.

I jammed the cell phone at him, trying to catch my breath and my sanity. "Look at it."

David's face lost its color as he read the screen. "Who?" he asked.

"Don't know."

"When?"

"About twenty minutes ago."

"Where?"

"Parking lot at work. Just after I met with Paul."

I bent over, hands on thighs, realizing I was hyperventilating and working to get level–headedness back into my brain. There was a loud knock on the laundry room door off the kitchen, followed by a "Hello?"

I lifted my head at the familiar voice just as David gave me a look that said *Are you kidding me?*

Paul walked in, looking as rattled as I felt. "You left the doors open," he said, jamming a thumb in the direction he came. "I figured it was okay to come in."

David shot me another look but I let it pass. Now wasn't the time.

He pulled out his own cell phone from his jeans pocket, keyed in a bunch of numbers and turned all business when the connection went through. "Nat, come over. Now." He disconnected and dialed again and as he waited through the rings, he started to curse. "He works at a goddamned phone company," he complained under his breath, "and he doesn't even pick up the goddamned phone." When the connection went through, he fired off his demand. "Neil, it's David. Call me ASAP." Then he turned back to me. "Give me all the details."

I shared a quick glance with Paul, deciding I'd give David only the most important ones. I left out the part about possibly seeing Mrs. Reynolds. When I finished, David's expression looked darker and more threatening than before.

"You should know that Jim McKarren called while you were out." David's tone didn't sound promising. "Like Nat, his search on the florists came up with nothing linked to you or this address."

"But there's a connection," I said, stating the conclusion we'd both been considering all along.

David nodded.

My breathing started coming in fits again and I moved to the slider, leaning my head against a cool pane of glass with an irrational goal of finding more air.

I felt someone slip in behind me and heard Paul's voice in my ear. "Focus on your breathing. Tune into the sensations of the cool and the warm. When the unsettling thoughts come, let them drift away without judgment or emotion." He breathed out loud and in time with me, keeping me in rhythm and in sync, then his voice dropped even lower. "Focus. Let go, and focus."

David sighed, disturbing the moment, and I captured his reflection in the slider. He was sitting on one of the leather chairs with my cell phone in hand, searching through it. For what, I wasn't sure. The front doorbell rang.

"Unlocked!" David called out, and Nat trekked in.

"What gives?" he asked David. "Sounded like you were having a coronary when you called."

"Check this out," he said, handing Nat my phone. "This was sent to Lottie about thirty minutes ago."

Nat read the text, whistled and looked at me. "You got a way with people, you know that?"

I left Paul's reassuring presence and headed toward David.

"I need you to check out the Amrose parking lot," David told Nat. "See if you can find traces of someone watching Lottie."

I realized I couldn't withhold what might be important information from them any longer. "I think I might have seen someone there."

David stilled. "Who?"

"I'm not sure. It might have been Mrs. Reynolds."

"What?" Paul asked.

"I didn't see her for sure. It looked like a woman with blonde hair. But then I thought I saw a woman with dark hair." I leaned against the sofa and rubbed my forehead. "I'm not sure who or what it was. It could have been a memory. I don't know. I just don't know."

"Calm down, Lottie," Paul said. "I'll get you some water."

"Did you have another episode?" David asked.

"No. It wasn't like that. I was sitting in my Jeep, thinking, and then I thought I saw someone walking in the woods. When I got out to check, no one was there."

"It could have been a hypnagogic hallucination," Paul said, handing over an open bottle of spring water.

I took a few sips. "I was thinking, Paul, not imagining things while falling asleep." I glanced at Nat. "What about calling the police?"

Nat looked at me like I'd lost my mind. "What about no?" He leaned in and planted a kiss on my cheek. "Don't you worry, little lady. We'll get this figured out for you."

I nodded, more with hope than agreement. At this point, I'd give anything to have one clue. Just one.

Nat took off just when David's cell rang. It was Neil, and David once again asked him for help. As David explained the situation, I took a seat on the sofa. Halfway down, my legs gave out and I collapsed onto the cushion, battling a hefty and sudden dose of fatigue and dizziness.

Paul settled in beside me. "You feeling sick?"

I nodded.

David ended his call and sat on the armrest on my other side, pressing the back of his hand to my forehead. "She's clammy again."

"Tell me what Neil said," I said, shutting my eyes, but the heavy blackness only made the dizziness worse. I refocused on David's concerned features instead.

David hesitated and I knew what he was thinking.

"No. No hospital," I argued, "and no doctor."

"Lottie, you're not being reasonable."

"I can help her if she needs it," Paul said. "She just needs to relax first."

David gave Paul a long, confrontational look.

"Trust me," Paul said.

David regarded Paul's request but I could see the uncertainty still lurking inside. Then he turned to me and answered my question. "Neil said that whoever sent those texts to you sent them from a burn phone. I got a name and number of the person who bought it, for cash according to the records, but I'm not holding my breath that it'll lead anywhere. People buy burn phones for only two reasons. Anonymity is one of them."

"What was the name?" I asked.

"John Smith."

"How original. Where did John Smith buy the phone?"

"Here's the really bizarre part," David said. "He bought it from the phone store in the Applewood Mall."

"That's fifteen minutes away from us." I brushed the hair from my face and dizziness rolled back in.

"She's losing color," Paul said.

"Let's get you upstairs and into bed." David braced me with a steadying grip on my arm and helped me to my feet. He went on about how he'd call a doctor if I didn't improve while Paul suggested that my disorder was more psychologically driven than physically, and that he intended to provide the therapy. I was vaguely aware of walking up the stairs when their voices turned more urgent and almost argumentative.

"There's no reason to fight," I told them.

"We're not even talking," David said.

But I'd heard the voices. I was studying and sitting beside a window, watching a group of young men in their military kilts conducting their drills near the army barracks in the distance, some sparring by hand and some becoming more familiar with the bow. None looked very agile or very skilled in the ways of war, and I guessed that they were in their first season of training, preparing much the way Bakari had done just after he turned thirteen and left for a career with the army.

"Shemei." Haji, my tutor, was waving a hand to grab my attention.

I batted him away so I could keep looking outside.

"Where is your head these days?" Haji asked. "You sit on your reed mat next to me and yet, somehow, you are not here."

Someone knocked on the inner wall to our room and both Haji and I turned. I sprang to my feet once I recognized the familiar face.

"Bakari!" My sandals slapped on the bright blue tile floor as I ran to greet him.

Bakari swept me off my feet and squeezed me, as happy to see me as I was to see him. His arms were strong, his chest wide and his legs and stomach were solid muscle. He had filled out a lot since I last saw him.

Haji pushed the papyrus studies off to the side and stood, but kept his distance. For some reason, he never liked Bakari and he never tried to hide the way he felt.

"I believe your lessons are over for the day," Bakari said to me, draping an arm around my shoulder and looking at Haji. "I have it on good authority."

"Whose?" Haji demanded.

Bakari grinned. "Mine."

"I do not think so. I am under instruction to care for her studies until Last Meal, and—"

"And her day ends now."

Bakari grasped my hand and tugged me through the doorway and into the spacious hall just outside, with limestone walls painted with yellow birds and floor tiles the color of green grass and a ceiling nearly as bright as the sun. Haji followed, but only far enough so that his voice could be heard.

"Do not expect that this behavior will be ignored!" he yelled.

"Like I care," Bakari muttered, and he squeezed my hand all the harder as he pulled me down granite stairs and then out into the brilliant afternoon light that reflected off the limestone–pillared courtyard.

We laughed as we ran down to the river, and when we fell onto the sand and wrapped ourselves around one another, I thought only one thing.

I belonged with this man.

And then I was no longer making love near a river but walking down the hallway toward the open doors of my bedroom. David directed me to our bed and helped me into it, and when my head hit the pillow, he kissed my cheek, felt my forehead again, and sighed.

Paul moved in just behind him.

"Want to get into something more comfortable?" David asked.

"No." I fluffed up the pillow, rolled onto my side and looked up at him. "I'm fine just like this."

David excused himself to get me some juice and a damp washcloth for my head, and once he disappeared from the room Paul stepped into his place.

"Don't look at me like that," I said to him.

Paul sat down on the edge of the bed next to me. "I think we should put off your therapy until tomorrow." He reached for the nightstand and handed me a small paper cup filled with water. I had no recollection of him going to the bathroom and getting it. "But it would be a good idea if you took this in the meantime."

He held out a small pill that I immediately recognized because I'd seen Paul prescribe them before. It was a sedative, and a strong one.

"I don't take those," I said.

Paul pushed the pill closer to my mouth, urging me to

change my mind. "It'll help you relax."

"Knock me out, is more like it. And since when do you carry these things on you, anyway?"

Paul ignored the question. "Take it."

I hesitated.

"Don't you trust me?" he asked.

"Of course I do."

"Then what's the problem?"

I hesitated but finally gave in and took the pill because I was just too tired to fight it.

"Where is your head these days anyway?" Paul asked.

He brushed a strand of hair from my face. It was a soothing gesture but I tensed at his words. They seemed familiar somehow. I had heard them before but they had been spoken with authority and a measure of impatience.

"You're here next to me," he said, "and yet somehow you aren't here."

I grappled with the memory as I let my eyelids close with the first effects of the sedative, the rational part of me telling me that taking it had been a mistake.

A wisp of an image of reed mats and papyrus scrolls and a window overlooking army barracks settled over me.

"Are you Haji?" I asked Paul, my voice sounding young and unsure.

"Go to sleep, Lottie," Paul said. "You need the rest more than you realize."

Chapter Twenty

I dreamt about Bakari, and a warm, balmy night in the Great Hall.

He leaned down and whispered in my ear. "There is no need to pretend with me, Shemei. I know what you want because I know you as well as I know myself."

Three seasons had passed since I last saw Bakari when he left for another war, and in that time he had become one of Pharaoh's most successful and influential soldiers. He wore a military kilt and a jeweled sword at his side and everything around us—the blue–tiled floor littered with hibiscus, the honeyed lamb and roasted gazelle, and the nude dancers who moved in time to the music—faded into the background.

"Want to leave?" Bakari asked with a conspiratorial look I had seen hundreds of times before.

"I do not know if we should. This celebration is for Egypt as much as it is for you. You were appointed General tonight, Bakari. You were instrumental in defeating another enemy, and I do not think Pharaoh would appreciate your disappearing on him."

"But I have a special jug of wine, just for us."

"Stolen wine?" I asked, pretending to be surprised.

Bakari grinned and moved in close enough for me to feel his body heat and a lot more. "Of course."

We slipped out from the celebration and made our way

through the trees and bushes that encircled the village, then over the hill to the special place by the Nile that Bakari found for us when we were children. We sat in quiet stillness for some time and while I admired the gleaming, starlit sky, Bakari seemed focused only on me.

His fingertips swept over my cheek and down to my chin, and his eyes caught mine and held. For a moment, I saw something in them that I had not seen before. Something that seemed softer. More tender.

Everything fell silent. It was only the two of us, eye to eye, heart to heart.

Bakari loosened the gold belt at my waist and slid the linen sheath from my shoulder. He kissed me once, then once again, and pulled me on top of him.

The wine was left in the soft grass nearby, unopened and forgotten.

The alarm went off and I jolted awake to see David in bed next to me. He was resting on his side with his head propped in a hand, watching me with the same hunger I'd seen in Bakari.

"That must have been one hell of a dream you were having." David pulled me to him and kissed me. His body burned and molded into mine, and what I saw in the depths of his eyes hinted at the sinful things he had in mind, too.

He kissed me again, dipping his head once to nip at my ear and whisper that, by the time he was done with me, I wouldn't be able to remember my name. I trembled in anticipation and, for a moment, I was back in Bakari's arms. He traced fingertips over my cheek, down my neck and toward my blouse. With a deft hand, he unbuttoned the top two buttons and slid inside. A moan escaped my lips as he did away with the blouse and followed with the bra.

"Clothes," I begged. "Get rid of all of them."

He shook his head and his mouth curved into a grin, and the evil lurking behind it sent a jolt of pleasure through my body. He rolled me on top of him, half-naked and insane with desire, and hiked up my skirt.

"I can't stand the arguing anymore," David murmured, snapping off my lace panties and flinging them to the floor, leaving nothing between me and every hard inch of him. "And I want things the way they were before. The way we used to be."

"Me, too," I breathed.

I straddled his body, amazed that even after all these years I never grew tired of looking at him, of feeling him, but in a moment of reason my body reminded me of other needs almost as important. "But I could use a few minutes to freshen up first," I said, and the words got mixed in with another moan as David's hand traveled downward and in between.

"After. We can take a shower together." He found the right spot and the first tremors of climax hung on the fringes. "Then we can do this all over again."

This was feeling way too good. Which wasn't a problem until my stomach growled.

David's mouth claimed mine once more, this time refusing to let go.

"I need to eat, David," I mumbled into his lips.

"So do I."

"I meant food."

Just as my head started spinning and I was getting into rhythm with David's hand, my stomach grumbled a second time. Loudly.

David brushed my hair off to the side and bit my neck. I gasped, caught between pain and pleasure. Somewhere in the recesses of my brain, my internal clock clamored for attention.

"What time is it anyway?" I asked, enjoying the feel of David's tongue as it played over the sensitive skin he'd just tortured.

"Who cares?"

"*David.*"

David stopped what he was doing, blew out a breath, and stared up at me, flushed and frustrated. He fumbled for the clock on his nightstand and said, "It's just before six." Then his teeth grazed over the other side of my neck before inflicting delicious pain there, too.

I moved a little to the side, wanting more and thinking about how I was going to torture him in return. "What about that new Thai place?" I kissed David's chest. Felt his heart beating with mine. "We could order for delivery."

David froze. "It's just before six in the *morning.*"

It took a few seconds for the message to sink in. I shoved off and grabbed the clock, needing to see for myself. "I've been out for *sixteen* hours? This is why I hate those pills." I sat up, irritated that I'd lost so much time and angry that I let Paul convince me to take one in the first place. "They knock me out in the worst way."

"Is that such a bad thing?"

"Yes," I said. "It is."

"Does this mean we're not having sex?"

I made a frustrated noise and went to the bathroom for a quick break, feeling agitated and still aroused.

"So you had some extra sleep," David called out. "What's the big deal? You obviously needed it."

I came back and climbed into bed. "No, David. I *didn't* need it."

David considered me for a few long seconds. "Do you really want to do this right here? Right now?"

Not really.

"That's what I thought," David said, and it wasn't until he pulled me back on top of him that I realized I'd said it out loud.

Then his cell phone rang.

The interruption was met with David's loud, infuriated curse. He inspected caller ID, cursed again and mouthed, "It's my CO. I have to take this."

In less than twenty seconds the call was complete. In less than five I'd found out that David had a meeting at seven at headquarters, and in less than three that he intended to finish what he'd started between us.

"I thought you were off for a couple of weeks," I said.

"This is just for today."

"And you have to be at PROs in an hour."

"We'll make this quick," David said, throwing his phone to the floor. "Quicker if you talk dirty."

"I could do that. My first client isn't until eight."

David went still.

I sat up, confused and overheated. "What's wrong?"

David's expression changed into one that many women knew well. One that said he'd done something wrong and that he expected to pay hell for it. He hitched himself up on his elbows and said, "Paul talked to Stuart Hanley at Amrose and canceled your appointments for the rest of the week because you're still sick."

"He talked to Amrose's director and did what?" I pushed off David, snagged the sheet and covered myself. The phone call may have put a temporary freeze on the mood but this latest news made it as good as dead and buried. "And you let him?"

David's silence confirmed my suspicions.

"I can't believe this." I started pacing the room. "You actually made these decisions without my input. About *my* clients. *My* workday. *My* life." I rounded on him and stared him down. "What were you thinking?"

David sat up, his expression one of complete calm. A defense mechanism, I realized, to avoid a full–scale, all–out argument. "I was thinking about your safety."

I couldn't think straight. My blood pressure pounded in my head and it took considerable effort not to call David every name I could think of. And then I would have followed up with Paul.

I gritted my teeth, working hard to keep my rising temper under control. "I am *not* a child, David. I am perfectly capable of making these decisions on my own."

David got out of bed, not once breaking eye contact. "Someone threatened you yesterday. You heard voices that no one else could hear. You're still having episodes—"

"Memories—"

"And *I* am perfectly capable of making decisions that involve your safety."

"You don't own me, David."

David threw his arms up in frustration. "This has nothing to do with owning anyone!"

"And I could have made this decision on my own!"

David's voice grew louder and deeper. "Someone is out there," he said, jabbing a thumb at the windows, "watching you and preparing to attack you or worse. When are you going to get it through your head that this isn't a game?"

"And when are you going to get it through your head that you can't think for me?"

"Since when is it a crime for me to care about my wife's well–being?"

We were both stunned into silence, not because of how loud he'd bellowed but because he'd unintentionally breached the agreement we made years ago regarding marriage.

Now that the slip–up had been made, there was no ignoring it.

"I'm not going to apologize for that," he said, and his voice trembled under the weight of long–concealed discontent.

And I wasn't sure how to handle it.

"So much for going back to what we used to be," he said, grabbing his clothes from the floor. "I'm heading out to work. Do what you want. You're going to do it anyway."

He disappeared inside his closet to get dressed. As a psychologist, I knew our immature behavior was going to make our relationship even more strained. As David's lover, I feared it could damage our relationship in a way that might not be fixable.

I drew in a ragged breath, annoyed and angry that I'd let the situation get so out of control. I was simply tired of feeling like everyone controlled my life except me.

David stalked out of the closet in jeans and a T–shirt and running shoes, snagged his keys and wallet off the dresser and headed downstairs without a word. A pang of regret lanced through my heart as I heard the garage door rattle open and shut.

"What's happened to us?" I asked the empty room.

When I finally decided stewing about the fight would do me no good, I decided to shower and dress, but when I was done getting ready I had no idea what to do with the rest of the day. Or the week, for that matter. I thought about talking with Stuart Hanley and changing his mind, but once Stuart made a decision there wasn't much someone could do to change it. Then I had another idea.

I set the house alarm, got in my Jeep and stopped at a Starbucks on the way to Amrose. When I got to the office building and stepped out of the air–conditioned car and into the parking lot, the heat and humidity slammed into me like an oppressive wall. I wandered through the parking lot and through the treed area that encircled it, disregarding the sweat that trickled down my back and dampened the brown linen dress I wore. I thought I'd seen Mrs. Reynolds the day before but I still wasn't sure, so I had no idea what to look for or what clues would jump out at me. It didn't matter that Nat had already been here yesterday, doing the same thing. I needed to see for myself, and to finally take control.

As I made a second pass around the parking lot, the rich, spiced scent that I now knew so well drifted in. I stopped and inhaled, and had a sudden, vague memory of a man with sand colored eyes.

"Doctor Morgan?"

Galen was standing next to me.

My first reaction was to run but something about him told

me my fears were unwarranted. I remained where I stood, wary and watchful.

"What are you doing here?" I asked.

"I should ask the same of you."

The breathtaking scent blossomed and intensified.

I cleared my throat and said, "I work here."

Galen slid his hands into his pockets. "Not for the rest of the week, I believe."

I pulled away, my wariness kicking up a few notches.

"I have the answers you need, Doctor Morgan."

I swayed where I stood, spellbound by that stirring, intoxicating aroma. "You understand what I've been experiencing?"

"Yes."

"And you can help me?"

"Yes."

I hesitated, and my cell phone rang. I had a distant thought that I should answer it, but I was tangled up in an image of the two of us. Together.

The phone rang again.

"Take it," Galen said. "It may be important."

But I couldn't move.

Galen tugged the phone out of my bag and handed it over. "It might be a client."

It was Logan.

"I need your help, Doctor Morgan. Right away."

He sounded winded and anxious and my head cleared when I realized something was wrong. "Where are you? What's going on?"

"I'm outside your house and I need to see you." There was

a shuffling sound, broken by another urgent plea. "Please come now. I think they're watching me."

Before I could ask anything else, Logan disconnected the call.

"Our conversation will have to wait," I said to Galen. "Sorry."

I jumped into my Jeep, sped home and raced up the driveway, jamming to a stop just outside the garage. I leapt out and scanned the front lawn. No Logan. I ran around the side of the house, checked the backyard and wound up on the front lawn again. Still no Logan. Sweating and bewildered, I ran to the curb and checked up and down the street.

Nothing.

My mind raced with too many unanswered questions and lots of doubts. I ran up the front steps and unlocked the door, desperate for air conditioning and ready to make phone calls, and as soon as I crossed the threshold another unbidden image assaulted me. One of a jeweled sword arcing down to kill me.

I bent over and clenched my stomach over a sharp stab of pain. A pair of hands grabbed me.

"Don't fight me," Galen said. "This will go much more easily if you do what I say."

He closed the door and locked us both inside.

Chapter Twenty-One

"Who are you?"

I backpedaled through the foyer toward the den. Galen followed.

"You already know," he said.

The back of my legs bumped into one of the leather chairs and I held up a hand. "Stay there."

Galen stopped. "I can help you," he said. "You're fighting what has been happening to you and that will only hurt you in the long run."

"Stop that," I said.

He held out his hands. "There is no need to be afraid. I won't come any closer."

"It's not that. It's your voice. It..." It coursed through my veins like heady, red wine. "It does things to me."

Heat radiated between us and the first luscious beads of sweat broke out on my neck and chest. Galen's eyes dropped to the bare skin revealed by my low cut dress and stayed there.

Run, a little voice inside insisted.

Galen's eyes lifted and found mine once more, and the spark of something dark and daring lit inside them.

"We know each other," I said.

"*Knew* each other."

"How?" I stepped around the sofa, needing physical distance from this man as much as emotional balance. "I see these memories of you and me, but I don't understand them. They've been coming too quickly for me to make sense of them, but I know you see them, too. Please tell me what's happening."

"I can guide you but I cannot tell you, Doctor Morgan. You must find most of the answers for yourself."

"Then why did you follow me here?"

"I had my suspicions about who you were when I saw you at the bar on Friday night," he said, "but knew only for certain when we met for my evaluation."

I nodded even though I didn't understand, the rhythmic cadence of his voice caressing my skin and stirring long–forgotten memories of the two of us, entangled in each other.

"What do you remember?" he asked.

I told him, and it was very little. "I see snippets of you and me. And I've seen David, too. But none of us are who we are now."

A sad smile emerged on Galen's lips. "No. Those times are gone."

"I want to know about those times, Galen. No one believes what I'm seeing and I want to know. I need to know." Otherwise, I was afraid I'd lose my mind.

Galen gestured to the sofa. "May I sit?"

"Were we lovers once?"

"For a very brief time, yes."

Galen sat and looked at me, and again I was drawn into those unusual eyes that held too many secrets and too few answers. I felt the pull of him, of what we were, and found myself moving closer to him as if my legs had no will of their own. I sat down but couldn't bring myself to look at him.

"Shemei," he whispered. The name rushed through me like a breeze over sand dunes, and his fingers swept my face and settled on my chin. "You have her cleft chin. And her heart–shaped birth mark on your shoulder." I pulled away, feeling naked and vulnerable and wondering if I had made a mistake by letting this go on. "You have her eyes, and her skin. Her voice and her scent. It is truly remarkable how very similar you are." He dropped his hand and whispered the name again. "Shemei."

He made it sound beautiful, like the wisp of a warm, summer breeze.

"Tell me about her," I said.

Galen took his time to think about what he was going to say. "You were Pharaoh's sister. And Bakari was his General. I served under Bakari for many military campaigns."

"I remember that. He went away very often." Sometimes months and months at a time.

And though it was Galen who was with me now, I sensed Bakari's presence nearby. Saw the devilish grin and playful green eyes that found him too much trouble as a child, and heard the deep, commanding voice that spurred his men into action as an adult.

"Bakari was a very powerful and successful soldier, devoted to his Pharaoh and to the throne. He was one of Pharaoh's primary confidants." Galen paused again, longer this time. "He was also hopelessly in love with you."

I sensed a subtle shift in Galen's mood that I didn't understand, but when I searched his expression to find the reason behind his jealousy, he pressed his lips together and turned away.

"I have so few memories of Bakari right now." I got up and went to the slider and watched a breeze ripple over the pool. An image of the Nile, glittering like thousands of diamonds beneath brilliant starlight, surfaced. Bakari and I were alone by the Nile in our special place, drinking stolen wine and finding each other. "I see some of our childhood together and moments from when we became lovers. And I remember a servant. But other than that, I see only you, Galen. Mostly you. And nothing more." I turned and faced him. "Why?"

"Your regression is probably incomplete. You must give it time."

"But you know what I lived through. I can see it on your face."

"I did not live your life. What I see is only through my eyes and my experiences, not yours. For me to tell you about how you lived your life would be unfair."

"You can tell me something. Things we did together, or said to each other. Experiences that we shared."

"I could."

"You said you could help me, Galen, and now you're shutting down on me. If anything is unfair, that's it."

I grabbed his arm to demand the truth, but when my skin touched his other memories exploded in my mind.

Garlands made of lilies and lotus hung from the tiled ceilings and wrapped around each sculpted column. Flower petals of blue and green and yellow adorned each table as well as the reed mats beside them. Servant girls tied floral collars of chamomile and green leaf on guests, and empty wine jugs spilled over with blue and white lotus. Women poured cinnamon–spiced wine into cups and others served trays filled with dried fish, figs and dates, thick loaves of bread, and seasoned beef. I stood in a crowded room where people cheered as my brother and his generals distributed weapons to the soldiers that marched through. People ate and drank, women danced and shook sistrums, and music played long into a night that promised future success and everlasting glory.

After the last soldier passed through, I excused myself from my table in need of fresh air. Although the night was warm it was not uncomfortable and, for once, a cooling breeze blew through. At the edge of the granite balcony, I closed my eyes and relaxed under the gentle wind, allowing the effects of the wine to quiet my senses.

"It is a magnificent night, is it not?"

I did not need to look to know who had joined me. His voice warmed my blood as much as the wine did. "It is," I said to Kemnebi. "And the restfulness it offers seems out of balance to the trials that are coming for Egypt."

Kemnebi nudged my arm and when I opened my eyes he held up two cups of wine, offering me one.

I hesitated.

"It is from my vineyard," Kemnebi said in an attempt to sway my decision, "which Pharaoh sees fit to drink from quite often. In fact, those at his dais are among the only ones tonight who are enjoying it. I would like you to enjoy it, too."

He offered the cup again and moved in next to me on the balcony. The wine looked as rich and red as the darkest pomegranate, with three blue lotus petals floating on top. I took the cup but did not drink.

Much to his credit, Kemnebi did not try to sway me again.

"What a remarkable view," he said instead, taking a sip and then one more. "The temple seems to glow with the newborn moonlight, does it not? Even the Nile glitters, as if filled with shining jewels."

I nodded but it seemed all I could do. I was having a hard time focusing on the view, the wine, even the night itself. His voice stole every thought from my head. Had command over every reaction in my body. It seeped through me and merged with me until I no longer felt we were two people but one.

I moved away, needing space. This, whatever this was, felt dangerous and wrong.

Kemnebi glanced my way, the trace of a grin playing on his lips, the darkness in his eyes drawing me into a place I had never been before. A place that harbored secrets and promised danger.

A place I had to avoid.

Kemnebi moved in closer and I stood motionless. His eyes scanned my hair, my face, my lips, and went lower still.

"My lady?"

The moment Kemnebi and I shared shattered, and in silence I thanked the gods for the intrusion. I straightened, put my cup on the granite ledge and turned to my servant, Kesi.

"I am sorry to interrupt, my lady. Pharaoh is summoning you." She looked from me to Kemnebi and back to me again, eyes alert and as if she were putting this moment into memory. "Shall I tell Pharaoh that you are detained with someone else?"

Her accusatory tone and critical eyes made me pause. "No," I said, and without looking back I returned to the Great Hall. My brother was talking with several soldiers near the dais and when he saw me he motioned for me to join him. As I approached, Bakari appeared from behind and we walked toward the dais together. My brother snapped his fingers and several attendants banged on wine jugs to quiet the crowd. Once the room hushed, my brother stepped up on the dais, commanding the attention of everyone there.

"Promising occasions such as tonight can only serve as a prelude of others to come," he said. "So it is with great pleasure and delight that I announce the upcoming marriage of my sister, Princess Shemei, to General Bakari."

The room erupted into applause and my brother looked down at Bakari. "All the more reason for success in our next battle, General, because now, more than ever, you have something to come back home to." He raised his cup in salute to everyone in the Great Hall. "To Shemei and Bakari!"

A chorus of hundreds echoed his toast. "To Shemei and Bakari!"

Bakari and I kissed and wove through the celebration to make our exit, stopping along the way to accept everyone's good wishes and for Bakari to grab a jug of wine hidden behind a flowered column. I laughed when he presented it to me. No night with Bakari could ever truly be special without stolen wine.

At first I thought we would head back to my chamber but the gods seemed to have other plans. We bypassed the royal court and climbed over a steep hill, heading for our secluded sanctuary by the Nile. Re had long since descended in the sky, which was now filled with thousands of gleaming stars, some of which looked as if they were falling right to the ground.

"I wonder what that means," I said, sitting down on the thick grass and pointing to one that blazed in a bright, burning arc before disappearing altogether. "Why would the gods throw themselves across the sky like that?"

Bakari sat down beside me, popped the seal on the wine jug, took a long sip and handed it over. "Maybe they are happy and cannot sit still."

I drank some wine and smiled at the thought. "A good omen, then, for Egypt."

Bakari took the jug and put it off to the side. "I was thinking more of a good omen for us. And for our life together after I return from this next campaign."

He pulled me on top of him, slid off my sheath and molded the two of us together. His skin felt hot, his body ready, and when he slid inside me we both stilled.

"From childhood you have been everything to me, Shemei," he whispered. "Only now, more so. For all of eternity, you will be here." He pressed my hand to his heart.

We made love under the stars that night, languorous with each touch, impassioned by each promise made, stopping only to quench our thirst with stolen wine before taking pleasure in each other once again.

Later, after we were spent, we dressed and paid homage to Re and his Immortal Barque as it ascended into a new day.

Bakari took my hand in his. It was time for him to leave for war.

Another emotion rushed in to follow, this one filled with grief and sorrow. Flashes of other images also came, all fleeting and raw.

I was racing through paths and alleyways and over roads and hills, converging with thousands of other Egyptians with the same goal in mind. The mob shouted out for all our glory, and down the sphinx–lined Avenue I spotted the royal litter with my brother seated in its center, the war crown steady on his head.

My servant, Kesi, was at my side, standing on her tiptoes, her cheeks red with excitement. "They are coming! They are coming!"

The first division of soldiers arrived, and the other three divisions descended over the sandy hills just behind. Chariots filed in on either side of the Avenue, displaying the gold and armor and weapons and jewels acquired from the campaign.

I forced my way through the chanting crowd, needing to be up front, wanting to see and hear and share, firsthand, their victory. My brother scanned the mass of people from his litter and smiled when he found me, but his smile looked weary and bittersweet. His victory, it seemed, did not come without difficulty.

As the divisions continued marching in, I looked for Bakari. I leaned forward, trying for a clearer view, and felt someone tap my shoulder.

It was Kemnebi. My gaze dropped from his drawn, fatigued face to the object he held in his hands. It was a sword. A jeweled honorary sword.

"I am sorry, Shemei," he said, handing it over. "Bakari did not make it home."

The memory slammed shut like a heavy door and Galen's image slid back into place.

"You are Kemnebi," I said, testing the name out for the first time, and it felt awkward on my lips. "You're who I've been seeing all this time, as Kemnebi."

Galen nodded.

Too many questions came at me, all demanding answers at once. I tried reining in the rambling thoughts, trying to figure out what to ask next, and then next, but the harder I tried, the more overwhelmed I became.

"How is it that I can I see these memories but David can't?"

"Bellotti is not ready, so he does not understand."

"But he and I were lovers once, just like you and I were. Why can you and I see this? And why do I see this now, at this time in my life?"

"I do not know, Shemei."

I went to the photos of David and me on the fireplace mantle and fingered one of the two of us at Crested Butte when we went skiing last year. "He's turned you down three times for a spot on his team. Is it because of something that happened in the past?"

"He does not trust me."

"You didn't answer my question," I said, facing him. "Is it because of you and me?"

Galen took his time to respond, and in those silent seconds he seemed to struggle with admitting either the words or something deeper still. He glanced away and swallowed, and I realized he was battling guilt. And a lot of it.

"Yes," he admitted. "Bellotti's feelings about me exist on a level he can't quite grasp. It is definitely because of us that he does not trust me."

"But he doesn't know." I motioned to the space and the world around us. "No one seems to know. Or understand. Why?"

"That I cannot answer. Why does one person understand

the entire cosmos while another can only appreciate the moon? Why does one man see energy in a storm while another sees destruction?"

I thought about the things I knew, about the emotions and thoughts and actions of a lifetime so long ago, and felt a sudden loneliness. If I couldn't share the excitement over learning about it with David or Lori or Paul, then what was the point in knowing at all?

I looked to Galen for the answer and found it in his eyes. They beckoned to me, hinting of mysteries I wanted so desperately to understand. If no one else could give that to me, then I had to pursue it from the one person who could. I was determined to find the truth. *My* truth.

I walked to Galen and, instead of settling on the sofa beside him, lowered to my knees at his feet as if it were a natural and commonplace thing to do.

"What were we to each other?" I asked.

"We were everything that was good," he said with slow, measured words, "and everything that was bad."

There was something in his voice that sounded sorrowful, even contrite. I felt drawn to that pain, wanting to know why it existed and where it came from. I wanted to understand it because that pain, I knew, linked to me.

I reached out to him and touched his cheek. His skin was hot under my fingertips, like the sun that blazed over Egyptian sands. He drew in a sharp breath and held it, and his restraint emboldened me into further discovery. I caressed his face and wandered to his shoulders and across his well–developed chest. His shirt, I realized, was the same texture and color as my dress. A luxuriant, dark brown linen.

I moved to his arms, which felt lean and hard, and down to his hands. They were strong but I knew they could also be gentle. I remembered how they touched me and pleasured me. How they embraced and stroked, tormented and teased.

I became lost to the images of the two of us, tangled in soft, linen sheets, straining for release, reckless and distracted and uncontrolled. The rich and, by now, familiar scent emerged. The scent belonged to us, I realized, of when we were one.

In my head I heard his voice. The tempting, alluring lilt in the way he spoke. The calming effect his words had on me. The way he encouraged with promised whispers and soft murmurs.

I moved to his hard thighs and higher still, wanting more, needing to feel more, to remember more.

"Shemei," Galen said over a ragged breath. "You have to stop."

He grabbed my hands and pulled them away but my lust lingered. I was overheated and overpowered and all too aware that my intentions, curious and innocent as they may have begun, now hovered on something that could turn very wrong.

And then another voice cut in. "What the hell is going on here?"

Chapter Twenty-Two

The moment splintered under David's absolute and potent displeasure.

Galen withdrew to stand near the end of the sofa. I looked up at David and found myself on the receiving end of a punishing look that wanted any excuse for release.

"It's not what you think," I said in an attempt to diffuse his temper and its aftermath if left to run unchecked. "But I need your open mind again, David." I unfolded from the floor and stood. "Can you do that?"

He considered my request and me, and sent Galen an unspoken but all too clear message.

Galen picked up on it right away. "I found your wife at Amrose," he offered in explanation, and David didn't react to the mistaken assumption he made about our relationship. "I didn't receive any message that our meeting had been canceled until it was too late, but she received a phone call that upset her while I was there. So I followed her home to make sure she was okay."

"Galen shares my memories, David." I rushed to his side, hoping he'd join in my excitement. "It's exactly as I told you. What I remember was real because it happened. It was a part of another life, a past life between you and me that Galen was a part of, too."

David didn't say anything.

I used his silence to my advantage. "I lived as Shemei, and Galen lived as Kemnebi. He served under you when you were a General. You and I knew each other since we were children, just like we did in this life, David. We were going to be married, but then you went off to war and you didn't return. And then Kemnebi and I had a relationship after your death. These memories are real, David. They really, truly happened."

But as much as I tried to convince David, I could tell he'd already shut down. And I shouldn't have been surprised, either. Galen had been right on point when he made the comparison of one man understanding the cosmos while another could only appreciate the moon. For whatever reason, David was not meant to share in this revelation and that saddened me.

"Tell me what you're thinking," I said, because overly long silence from David never meant anything good.

"Perhaps I should leave," Galen said.

I held up a hand and stopped him. "No. It's okay."

Galen regarded David and interpreted his silence as a command. "I think it would be best if I did," he said, starting for the foyer.

David stepped in front of him, blocking his path. He had a few inches on Galen as well as more muscle, and he used his stature for outright intimidation. Galen, however, did not back down.

"I don't trust you," David said, and the menace in his voice and on his face became all too evident. "I'm willing to let it go—this time—and that's only for Lottie's sake. But give me any reason to question you again, *any* reason at all, and I will have you permanently removed from PROs. Is that understood?"

Galen nodded, gave me one final glance, and left.

"This wasn't Galen's fault," I told David when the front door closed. "He didn't deserve the brunt of your anger."

"Then he'll have to learn to live with it."

"You're not being fair—"

"I came home and found you with another man, and you're talking about what's fair?"

"And how many times do I have to tell you that it wasn't what it looked like?"

David took a stunned step backward. "Do you have any idea how weak that excuse sounds?"

"Yes, but it's the truth!"

I needed to take my own step back because I knew that if I let my anger run free, we'd launch into a heated and immature argument. When I found some kind of composure, I said, "Blame me if you need, but don't blame Galen. He's the only person who understands what I'm going through because he's experienced it himself. I can learn from him, David."

David stood firm and silent.

And I was going to test our relationship even further.

"I intend to meet with Galen again." David was ready to argue but I cut him off. "I need this because he's the only person who can help me. Maybe you can't put your trust in him but you'll have to put your trust in me. Otherwise, we should call it quits now because there will be nothing left for us to build our relationship on. And me not being your wife will be the least of your concerns."

For the first time in a long time, I'd left David stunned and speechless. I felt for him and understood his unsettled emotions, and I would have done anything to make them go away. The gods only knew I'd experienced enough of that very same confusion over the past few days myself, but I was determined not to back down.

"For what it's worth, and whether you choose to believe it or not," I said, moving in closer to him, "the history that Galen and I have doesn't compare to what you and I shared back in time, or what we share now."

David's eyes explored mine and I watched him battle uncertainty as well as pride.

"Come on, David," I said. "Work with me here. You know there's middle ground. We've found it before and we can find it again."

"You can't be serious," David said, his expression hovering somewhere between shock and disgust. "You absolutely cannot be serious."

Any hope of reconciliation took a backseat when my cell phone rang. I found it in my bag by the sofa, and answered.

"Doctor Morgan?" It was Logan and he sounded panicked. "I tried meeting you at your house but couldn't. Can you meet me at the Applewood Mall instead?" The sound of cars rushing past filtered through the connection. "There's something here you need to see."

I agreed and updated David once I disconnected.

"The Applewood Mall," I said. "Why does that sound familiar?"

"Because the person that texted you before bought the burn phone there." David checked my caller ID. "Take a look at this," he said, pointing to the screen. "It's also the same number of the person who called you the other day."

"Well, isn't that interesting." I hoisted my bag over my

shoulder and headed for the garage.

David grabbed my arm and stopped me. "We aren't done here, Lottie. We *will* talk about what happened later."

The hard, angry look in his eyes made me pause, but only briefly. "Good," I said. "I want that, too."

David took my Jeep keys, put them on the counter and retrieved his keys from his jeans instead. Then we both headed for his SUV with one goal in mind.

To follow what looked like our very first clue.

Chapter Twenty-Three

We got into the SUV, pulled out of the garage, and David fell into a deep, brooding silence. It wasn't his normal silence either. This one seemed edgy and hostile and directed at me.

"I think we need to talk now and not later," I said. "Things haven't been right between us since Galen left our house and we need to resolve it."

We came to a stop sign and David made a left, bringing us through the tree–lined, landscaped back roads of our neighborhood.

"I don't want to get into it right now," David said.

"Why not?"

We made another left and passed a row of condos all lined with boxwoods, deep red impatiens, and forest green lawns. David started drumming his fingers on the steering wheel. "Because it'll make things worse."

"Not necessarily."

David said nothing.

"Open and honest communication is critical to a relationship, David. You know that. It's why we made a promise not to lie when we reconciled two years ago. I realize that there are situations that may seem difficult or insurmountable, just like this one does, but honesty can make all the difference."

David's jaw clenched and I knew I'd struck a nerve.

"I know you're feeling conflicted over Galen, and that—"

David swerved to the shoulder and jammed the brake, and the SUV lurched to a stop.

"You think I'm *conflicted*? This isn't about conflict, Lottie. This is about the truth, just like you said, but you're the last person who should be flaunting it."

I pulled back at his sudden outburst. "What's that supposed to mean?"

David released his seat belt as well as his displeasure. "You want to know what I'm thinking? Then I'll say this plain and simple so there's no confusion and so that I don't have to repeat myself. I don't want you seeing Galen. Ever again."

I froze at the unexpected and, in my mind, outrageous demand. "I still haven't completed his evaluation."

"I don't want your evaluation. I don't want a file or notes or a recommendation. I want none of it. What I want is for him to stay out of your life, and mine."

He'd made his decision about Galen joining his team, I realized. And it was the same decision he'd made three times before.

"You're going to deny his request," I said. "Because of me. Because of what you think you saw between us."

"What I thought I saw?" David shook his head, adamant. "I didn't think anything. It was happening, right before my eyes, and the gods only know what would have happened next had I not walked in. Do you want me to get graphic, Lottie? Do you really want me to remind you of the details? Because I will if you need it. You may want to lie to yourself about this but you absolutely cannot lie to me."

I sat still, unable to defend myself because I couldn't

remember. I thought we'd stopped and that Galen pulled away before things got out of control.

Then again, maybe he pulled away because he knew David was there.

"I don't remember," I breathed. "I really, really don't."

David wanted none of my explanation. "How convenient."

"I'm sorry, and I'm trying to figure this out as much as you are. I just need your patience."

"You need patience now, too? Along with needing my open mind and, oh, needing me to ignore that your hand was inside another man's pants? Because that's a really good one. And what do I get in return, Lottie? A thank you and a kiss in gratitude?"

"Of course not!" I looked out the window, frustrated and exasperated. "I didn't intend for that to happen with Galen. It's just that these memories—"

"These memories. Yeah, I know. It's all about the memories."

I glared back at him. "What do I have to say or do to get this through your head? You think that on a whim I decided to sleep with someone just because I wanted to? You think I'm using Galen as an excuse to do it?"

"I don't know. Are you?"

"How could you possibly even think such a thing?"

"You tell me. You're the one who refuses to get married."

David stared me down and that's when I realized what had been bothering him all along. "This isn't about Galen at all. Or me," I said. "This is about *you*."

"No, Lottie, it isn't," David said over a defeated sigh. "And that's the point I can't seem to get through to you. It's about *us*. Our relationship, married or not, has always been about us. And today you let someone else in."

His disillusionment, so clear and so painful, wrenched my heart. I wanted to say so many things to make this right again, to take away his disappointment and mistrust, to say how sorry I was and to make him believe it.

But I didn't.

Because we both knew there was nothing left to say that would change his mind.

Chapter Twenty-Four

If we didn't have to make the trip to the Applewood Mall, I would have told David to turn around and go home. We pulled into the shopping center's parking lot and found a spot off to the right, where we sat watching people flitting into and out of the small stores.

"Do you see him?" David asked.

His tone sounded chilled and emotionless and I hated it. I shaded my eyes with a hand and scanned the strip mall, which was canopied by tall birch trees in full bloom, and found Logan in front of the phone store wearing high tops, jeans, a white beater, and a red ball cap, pulled down to his eyes. He shifted on his feet, cell phone in hand, spying people as they passed by. He appeared anxious and tentative, like he might have been worried that he'd be seen.

"There," I said, pointing him out.

We slid out of the SUV and walked over. Logan froze when he discovered I wasn't alone, sized up David and ran.

David ran after him.

They disappeared around the corner of the strip mall and I stood, sweating in the blistering heat. David had speed and power and I knew Logan wouldn't get far, but I wondered what would happen once he was caught. David would either drag him back to me or force answers out of him right then and there. Neither situation would be handled gently. And, for a brief moment, I regretted making the trip with David until I realized that a strong male hand was exactly what Logan needed.

A vague memory hung on the fringes. One of another time and another place. It was night, with a sky as dark as ink and a moon nearly as bright as the sun. People had encircled me and were pointing at me. I was being mocked. Many were demanding my death.

Bakari stepped forward from the shadows, a hand poised at the jeweled sword that hung from his military kilt. The moon reflected off its edge as he walked, the flickers of light cutting into the gloom that filled the royal court. For the first time since I knew him, his eyes did not appear bright green but instead looked a mournful gray. I had disappointed him and hurt him, and there was nothing I could say to undo the damage. I remembered appealing to Bakari for him to reconsider, but he had his orders. And he was going to obey them.

He drew up the heavy sword and one single tear rolled down his cheek.

Then the sword arced down, toward me.

I stumbled, losing the memory and my balance, and clutched my hand to my pounding heart. I didn't understand Bakari's rage and I didn't understand why the memory surfaced now. But I knew something was wrong.

A limousine pulled up to Giovanni's at the end of the strip mall, drawing my attention away from the lingering memory. Seconds later, a couple emerged from the restaurant and walked toward it. A breeze swept over the woman's long blonde hair and through her yellow, silk peasant dress, and I watched them say goodbye. There was a familiarity in their gestures and an intimacy that suggested something much deeper than friendship.

A wispy summer breeze passed through, carrying with it another memory.

I was looking for my tutor, Haji, because he had tasked me with a difficult translation that, he believed, would take me days to complete. I finished it in little more than one and was determined to show him that even though my head was often filled with thoughts of Bakari, I was perfectly capable of focusing on my lessons as well.

With the scrolls carefully tucked under my arm, I wound my way past pools of water lilies and lotus in the center of the royal courtyard, through a doorway and into a spacious hall just inside, with floor tiles the color of green grass that led to the room where I was tutored. The door to the room was not completely closed so I pushed it open just enough to see if Haji was inside.

He was sitting on his reed mat on the floor. Kesi was sitting on my reed mat next to him, her leg touching his. They spoke in hushed whispers and I wondered what they were doing. And why they were alone.

Then Kesi looked at Haji in a way that Haji's wife looked at him, too.

I did not know how long I stayed there, staring at the two of them, and just when I realized that I did not belong, Kesi glanced toward the door where I stood.

The memory shut down and I was back at Giovanni's. The man watched the limo pull away, and I used his preoccupation to quietly move in beside him.

"How long have you been seeing Mrs. Reynolds?" I asked Paul.

Paul spun around, shocked, and pasted on a smile as soon as he saw me. "I'm not seeing her. This is therapy."

"At a restaurant?"

He said nothing at first, not bothering to keep up with the lie but not bothering to admit the truth either. "I know what you're thinking," he finally said. "And you're jumping to conclusions over what you think you saw."

"The least you could have done was to tell me about your relationship with her, especially when you knew what I've been going through with Logan and his mother and that she intended to go into counseling with me."

"I didn't tell you because there was nothing to tell."

"Please don't lie to me. We've known each other far too long for that." I swiped the sweat off my forehead and the back of my neck and considered buying an iced cold drink to cool off.

Paul cocked his head. "Are you okay?"

"I'm angry," I said, lifting my hair and wiping the back of my neck again. "You lied to me, Paul, and you're still lying to me."

"It's not that hot out. Why are you sweating like that?" He reached out and I pulled away.

"I want to know what's going on between you and Mrs. Reynolds. Why are you even bothering to hide it?" I knotted up my hair, dug a tissue out of my bag and wiped down my skin. "You think I can't see what's going on?"

"There's nothing going on."

"I saw you with Kesi, in the chamber where you tutored

me. I saw you both together. Then, and now."

"What are you talking about? Lottie, you're not making any sense."

"What's going on here?"

David moved in between us and I fanned myself with the tissue. Sweat poured down my back, and my cheeks and chest flushed with perspiration.

"Lottie's feeling sick again," Paul said. "She's having another episode."

"It's too hot outside," I told David. "And the heat's getting the better of me."

"We're in the middle of a cold front, Lottie. It's only sixty–five degrees today." David pressed the back of his hand to my forehead. "You're not feverish, but you're sweating like crazy."

"She's acting confused," Paul added. "She doesn't seem to be operating in reality and is seeing things—"

"I know what I saw!" I argued.

"I think we should consider admitting her for observation," Paul said to David. "I thought maybe a week's rest from work might be good for her, but it's clear that there's something deeper at work here, and it needs immediate attention."

"No." I stepped away from them both. "I don't need a psych ward and I don't need a hospital. I'm fine."

David's gaze seized mine, sparking other images to life, all desperate and furious and brutal. I doubled over and clenched my stomach, fighting pain that tore through it. Darkness folded in, pulling me up and under until I knew death stood at my side. Something pressed down on my chest and with every ragged breath I drew in, the pressure deepened until I couldn't breathe anymore. Voices whispered in disapproval. Spectators closed in. Someone held me close and cried.

I saw the sword again, and pain lanced through my stomach.

I raced to a nearby bush and threw up.

David pulled my hair from my face and pressed a gentle hand to my back, waiting for me to finish. When I was done, he said, "I'm taking you to the hospital."

I yanked from his hold and held out my hands, cuing him to keep his distance. "No. No hospital."

"Lottie, you're sick."

I shook my head and started walking backward. "I'm not. You just don't understand what's happening because you can't see what I see."

David didn't argue and I didn't question why. Instead, I turned and kept going, unsteady at first but finding renewed strength with each step I took. By the time I reached the SUV, my body felt fresh and rejuvenated and as if nothing had happened. I drew in a long, satisfied breath while savoring a refreshing, cool breeze. The oppressive heat was finally gone.

A few moments later, David stepped into view. "You should know that I'm this close to throwing you over my shoulder and dragging you to the hospital anyway."

"The hospital can't help me," I said, turning to him. "There's only one person who can."

David's jaw clenched because he knew exactly whom I meant.

"You can either drive me to Galen's," I said, "or I'll find a way on my own."

It was a demand that bordered on threat but I had no

choice. I held my breath, waiting on his answer.

"Do you even realize what you're asking of me?" David asked, and the confusion and disbelief on his face ripped my heart in two. I'd never asked so much from the man I loved, knowing it could possibly destroy what we'd worked so hard to build between us.

"I need this, David."

His green eyes morphed into a murky, saddened gray. "More than you need me?"

"That's not what this is about."

"Isn't it?"

I shook my head. "No. Of course it isn't. Right now, I'm only asking for your trust and to believe in me. And in us."

David's anguished eyes searched mine, desperate for answers hidden deep inside me. Answers I knew I didn't have.

"Please understand me, David. *Please*."

I so wanted him to believe me, to finally realize that our love and our support would be enough to see this through. That we only needed time and patience, if he was willing to give it.

He paused, and for a few moments I thought that realization had finally come.

"I can't do this," he said. "I can't be a part of this anymore."

He handed me his keys, turned, and walked away.

Chapter Twenty-Five

I stood on the doorstep of Galen's brand new condo with a case of cold feet.

After David left, I took his SUV to Amrose to find Galen's address in my files, and it wasn't until I set foot on his property that I realized I didn't even know if he was home. I'd reacted defensively and without a plan and, if I was honest, knew that I made a terrible mistake with David as well.

Before I could turn and run or second–guess myself any further, Galen opened the door.

"I had a feeling you would come," he said. His eyes scanned the perimeter behind me. Out of suspicion, I realized.

"David's not here," I said. "I'm alone."

Making the admission made me feel vulnerable and exposed, and I said a silent prayer that I didn't make an error in judgment. Despite my memories, I'd known Galen all of several days and yet here I stood, placing myself at his mercy.

"I do not think meeting alone is a good idea," Galen said. "Bellotti made his intentions very clear about us earlier today."

I flushed with guilt and embarrassment at the reminder. "David knows I'm here, and I'm very sorry about what happened. I didn't fully realize what I was doing. It's just that," I paused, trying to grasp the riot of emotion and thought inside me. "It's just that you seem to be a very big part of me that I'm only starting to figure out now."

He pursed his lips in thought, and I remembered those lips curving over a cup of wine filled with blue lotus petals. He had brought the cup to his mouth and his eyes met mine as he sipped, and in his gaze I saw an unspoken promise of what was to come.

It was the same look in Galen's eyes now.

I drew in a breath and released it with the last bit of courage and dignity I had left. "I'm scared, Galen. I'm no longer sure who I am, and I'm scared of what will happen to me if I don't learn from you. I have no one else to go to."

He considered me a few seconds more. "We are dangerous together. You realize that, don't you?"

The suggestiveness in his voice wrapped itself around me like the finest linen, and I drew in another focused breath to fight it. "I know that. I also realize that we both risk something of great importance if we are not careful."

Galen nodded. "We were not capable of restraint back then, and I'm not convinced we are capable even now."

"I have no other choice. These memories are taking over and in a way that isn't healthy, and I'm running out of options."

At first Galen didn't seem convinced, then he stepped aside and motioned for me to come inside. Pretending courage I didn't feel, I followed him through a small foyer and into an open floor plan that included a den, dining room, and kitchen, and what I supposed were two bedrooms off to the side. I was surprised by the considerable size of the layout and even more so by the décor. Professionally designed in jewel tones and heavy, masculine woods, the rooms carried an air of elegance that suggested tasteful money. It wasn't until I gave the space closer inspection that I saw Galen's personal touches and understood why they were there. Framed Egyptian artwork. Replicas of faience pottery. Mirrors beveled with coral and lapis and ebony.

A vase filled with fresh blue lotus flowers.

I held back a gasp. "I received a bouquet like that just the other day."

"They are a favorite of mine," he said, glancing my way. "Though you probably already know why."

I nodded, and understanding came in a rush. "You sent those flowers to me," I said.

Galen nodded.

"Why?"

An odd look passed over his face, a mix of hopefulness and regret. "Once I saw you at the bar and realized who you were, I was intrigued and wanted to meet you. Then you collapsed so I followed the ambulance to the hospital to find out what happened." His expression dimmed. "Had I known at the time that you were married to Bellotti, I wouldn't have sent them. It was a mistake."

"We're not married," I confessed. "And considering how much you already know about me, I'm surprised you didn't know that."

A sentimental look passed over his face. "I know who you were, but not who you are now."

"When you were Kemnebi and I was Shemei, you mean."

"Yes."

My gaze traced the outline of his face, the line of his nose, the curve of his mouth. The mouth that, thousands of years ago, had kissed me and seduced me and encouraged me into doing things that should have been left undone. Despite my engagement to Bakari I had wanted him, and I found the excuse to have him.

Though I couldn't be sure, I had a feeling that the decision had cost me everything. And the words I'd whispered to him so very long ago I whispered again now.

"I do not want to want you."

Galen's eyes lit with quiet victory and I turned away, moving closer to the sofa and hoping the distance between us would settle my nerves and cool the attraction. "These memories come at me in waves and when I least expect them." I toyed with a pillow on the burgundy sofa and looked at him again. "Is that what happened to you?"

"No. My regression was much more difficult than yours seems to be. Bellotti triggered it when I met him for the first time about a year ago. It wasn't a pleasant experience."

"Why?"

He shrugged.

"My memories are clustering now, and they're starting to bleed into my present to the point that others think I'm losing touch with reality. It's like I can see and experience both lives at the same time and the harder I try to make everything fit, the less I understand. Did that happen to you, too?"

"Yes and no. You cannot force the memories to come, Shemei. You can only encourage them. That was my most difficult lesson to learn."

"A lesson from a regression therapist?" I asked.

"A regression therapist," he said with a wry smile, "cannot help your regression in the same way an actual person from your past can."

"Your experience must have felt very lonely."

"'Lonely' is not the word I would have chosen. And my experience was very different from yours."

He dropped his head, burdened by remorse that he didn't care to hide, and I marveled at the depth of emotion this man carried. David kept his feelings close to his heart, letting them out only when needed and with unconditional passion and intensity when he did. Galen wore his feelings like his clothes, visible to anyone who cared enough to pay attention.

"Do you know your entire past life now?" I asked.

"A good deal of it but not all of it."

He seemed disappointed by that, but not in a way I understood. "You make it sound as if learning about that other life was a mistake."

"In some ways it was."

"What happened to you?"

Long seconds passed by before he responded, and even then it seemed obligatory and with shame. "It isn't what happened to me but what happened to us."

"I don't understand."

Galen pressed his lips together.

I walked back to him and stood my ground. "I need to know, Galen. I have a feeling that what happened in my past is affecting decisions I'm making now. In fact, I get the feeling that it's not just my decisions that are impacted but also my life overall. There are parallels between these two lives and the people within it, and I don't understand what they mean."

"Because you are trying too hard."

In a single, fluid motion, Galen sat down on the sofa. His eyes met mine and I felt the familiar pull of his deep, extraordinary gaze. It seemed to hold so many secrets yet I sensed a distance in him that I couldn't comprehend. I suspected he kept that distance by choice.

"We were important to each other," I said, reading into his silence.

Galen nodded.

I sat down beside him. "Did we love each other?"

Galen didn't answer but I felt drawn into the emotional hold he had on me. Some instinctive, baser part of me recognized him, and somewhere deeper inside I felt a stirring passion that flickered and teased, needing only the right spark for it to burn again.

I searched his face, sifting through images and memories, the yearning and the desire, like the pages of a well–worn diary. In those soul–searching moments, a sudden awareness emerged and it was not the one I expected.

"You're the reason I can't commit to David."

Galen sighed and nodded.

"Because of an unresolved issue from long ago. From something I did with you."

"Yes."

I waited for more information but none came, and when I tried digging for the memories deeply buried inside me, the more out of reach they felt. It was like a cement wall had been erected, keeping me from what I needed to know.

"I need your help, Galen. Please."

"You already see what you need to see. You only need to open your eyes to understand. Let go of your fear, Shemei."

"I'm not Shemei, Galen. Not anymore."

"And that is why you can't move forward with your

regression. You're fighting the very person you are, deep inside."

The words seemed familiar, from a place that was lit with candles on a night that was filled with promise and unease. Galen had told me that I had lost Bakari to war, and I had invited him to my chamber wanting to forget the pain. Wanting to erase Bakari from my memory.

At least, that's what I had kept telling myself.

But once Kemnebi arrived, I wasn't sure I'd made the right decision. I wanted him to leave but I couldn't bring myself to make him go. In silence and solitude I stood near the bed I had only shared with Bakari, questioning what I'd done to anger the gods so much that they thought it necessary to take away the man I loved.

I felt Kemnebi's warm breath on my neck.

"Shemei," he whispered.

I turned to him and swayed on my feet as the first effects of the wine and the lotus took hold.

"Push me away, Shemei." His voice, as intoxicating as the flower and wine, flowed through my body. "Do it, or I will make the decision for us."

He pressed against me as his hands traveled lower. I felt the hunger and urgency in his body and when his mouth claimed mine, I tensed at the foreign taste of his tongue. The unfamiliar feel of his body on top of mine.

A body that was now Galen's.

"Galen!" I struggled beneath him, trying to break free. "Galen, please stop!"

Galen watched me through a clouded, faraway look and didn't respond. I wrestled out from under him, the shoulder strap ripping from my dress as I pulled free. He got up, swayed and moved for me again. I scrambled to my feet and shoved him, hoping to startle him out of his haze.

It didn't work.

"Galen!" I pushed him hard, then harder still. "Galen, snap out of it!"

I gave him one last push and slapped him, and Galen blinked as his cheek blossomed bright red. After a drawn out moment, he looked at me with clear eyes and sat back down on the sofa.

"I'm sorry," he said. "I don't know what came over me."

I forced him to focus on me, and the one question that still needed to be answered. "Tell me what happened Galen. I see something with David, with Bakari, and a sword. I know that sword ties in to you and me. Tell me what it means."

"I cannot."

"Why not?"

"Because if I do then I will tell you only what I want you to know, and that's just as bad as the lie I told you to make you think Bakari had died in battle."

"But I remember you giving me Bakari's sword after the war. You told me that he didn't make it."

"I told you he didn't make it but I didn't say that he died. You assumed that he did."

I stilled as the realization of what Kemnebi had done sank in. "You manipulated me and used me, knowing I would misunderstand your words when you returned from war."

"Not any more than you manipulated me that night."

I shook my head, adamant. "What I did was not the same."

"Look past your own ego and you will see that it is."

"You overpowered me. I stood little chance of fighting back."

"You fought well enough and you enjoyed it. Your despair over losing Bakari was just as strong as your desire for me."

"Bakari was my world."

Galen fixed me with a long, meaningful look. "Was he?"

I pulled back. "How could you even question such a thing?"

"You enjoyed the attentions I had always given you. You invited me back to your chamber the same night after you discovered Bakari was gone. If Bakari was your world, why did you encourage me? Why not wait until you had at least taken some time to grieve? Or at least ask the questions to confirm that Bakari was indeed dead?"

I couldn't answer because I didn't want to.

"It was all an excuse." Galen let that truth linger then added, "And I believe you're looking for another excuse now."

"I don't intend to sleep with you, Galen."

"Because Bellotti is your life?"

"Yes."

"And yet you cannot commit to him. Partly because of me but mostly because of you."

"I don't intend to betray David. I'm here for information, Galen, and to piece together memories. To find out what this all means. There's nothing more to it than that."

"Look at me and say that again like you mean it. I hear the words, Shemei, but they don't sound very convincing."

"You believe that because we slept together in a past life that we'll do it again?"

Galen moved in until we were breaths apart. "I believe you

are fighting your attraction now as you did then."

"That's ridiculous."

"If it is, then why do you flush every time you're near me? Why do you work harder at learning about your regression with me, and the life the three of us shared, and not with Bellotti? If you truly believe that Bellotti is your world," he asked, "then why did you invite me into yours?"

"I already told you why," I said.

"We are who we are. You're attracted to me as I was attracted to you back then, and you're still finding excuses to deny how you really feel." Galen leaned in and brought his lips to my ear. "We were very good together," he whispered. "Imagine what we could be if we had more time."

His voice was deep and rich and full of promise. His body was close. His mouth closer still. Vivid memories of the two of us came hard and fast. Our bodies moving together. An explosive climax. An insatiable physical addiction that drove us to near madness.

Galen was right. We were very good together. More than good together. And we could have those very same things again now. I only had to make the same decision I had made before.

It scared me that I could think such a thing, that I could even consider choosing someone other than David after all we had been through. It frightened me more how much I wanted it, how right and wrong it all felt, how my body felt so in tune with Galen's.

I only had to say yes.

Yes.

I cleared my throat, grabbed my bag, and left.

Chapter Twenty-Six

It was late afternoon by the time I pulled in my driveway, and I sat in David's SUV wondering if he was home and what his reaction might be once he saw my torn dress. Knowing I couldn't put off the inevitable, I unbuckled, turned off the engine, and headed inside.

I dropped David's keys near mine on the desk and saw no sign of David having been in the kitchen. No evidence that he'd even started the evening meal. The den also looked undisturbed and just as it did when we left earlier that day. Magazines and David's tablet were on the coffee table. The remote was on the sofa. The television was off.

Hefting my handbag over my shoulder, I headed into the foyer and for the stairs and considered calling David's cell when I heard a floorboard creak on the second story landing. I looked up and David looked down and we both stood in silence. He gave me the once–over before focusing on my ripped dress, where his eyes lingered for far too long. He frowned, pressed his lips together, and headed to our bedroom.

I stared at the empty space David had just occupied, thinking of all the different ways I could explain what he'd probably never believe. In the end, I decided maybe I shouldn't say anything at all. Sometimes people, especially those who needed to control, handled situations better when not encouraged to react, and this was one fire I didn't want to fuel.

By the time I reached the bedroom, David had disappeared. I dumped my bag on the bed and pulled out an orange tank top and white shorts from my dresser. David emerged from the walk–in closet just as I unzipped my dress and dropped it to the floor. He paused, mid–stride, his gaze moving from my face to my lace bra to my lace panties and back up to the bra again. A day or two ago he would have made a suggestive comment, or maneuvered me to the bed and seduced me. Today, judging by the look of disapproval on his face, I was the last person he wanted to see.

I held back a sigh. Maybe my decision not to bring up the dress had been the wrong one, and I would have said something about it but my attention went to the jeans and Nike shirts in his hands and the duffel bag on the floor.

"Are you packing?" I asked.

David turned from me and pulled out sport socks from the dresser along with several black tees. "Yes."

All the air escaped from my lungs and my knees gave out, and I sank onto the edge of the bed. Numbed by shock, I watched him pack until I could form only the simplest question in my mind.

"Why?"

He turned and looked at me again. "Please put on some clothes." He started shoving the tees into the duffel bag and zipped it closed.

I refused to let this happen. "We need to talk, David."

He sat on his haunches with his back to me and his shoulders slumped as if a crushing weight pressed down on him. "We've been doing a lot of that lately and it isn't getting us anywhere. There really isn't much left to say."

Except goodbye.

I quickly pulled on my tee and shorts and went over to him, ready to fight for us. "You couldn't be more wrong and you're assuming too much. We need to talk about you and me and Galen."

I watched David's back expand and contract with every deep breath he drew in. After what felt like too many drawn out seconds, he rose to his full height and faced me. "We've been through this already, Lottie."

"Yes, and I don't seem to be getting through."

"There's nothing to get through."

Like fine desert sand, I felt our relationship slipping through my fingers and scattering in all directions under the wind, with no hope of pulling it back into its original form.

Still, I wasn't going down without a fight. "How can I make you see? What can I do or say to make you understand that this is one miscommunication after another?"

He shook his head and let out a small, humorless laugh. "I see very well what's going on and I understand more than you give me credit for. In fact, I think I understand this situation better than you do."

"I don't think that's possible," I said, more sharply than I intended. "I don't want to fight about this, David. I just want to make things right between us again. Galen is—"

"Important to you."

I shook my head. "Not in the way you think."

David made a face that said it all. I wasn't fooling him even though I was trying to fool myself. He moved in closer and paused.

"You need to figure out who you are and what you want.

That's all it comes down to and that's why I need to leave."

He had made his decision and I couldn't change it. I swallowed over the growing knot in my stomach. "How long will you be gone?"

"A few days at least, maybe longer. It all depends." *On you* went unsaid. "I already know what I want and I've known for a long while now. The biggest disappointment for me is that I thought I knew what you wanted, too."

"Marriage."

"No," he said, shaking his head. "Me."

A dozen arguments surfaced in my head but David gave me no time to voice even one.

"At first I thought you didn't want marriage because of what happened with your birth parents," he said. "Or that maybe what you went through in foster care had scarred you. As much as not being married bothered me, it wasn't until Galen showed up that I realized it was much more than that."

With every word David spoke, I felt smaller and smaller still. The truth, painful as it was to hear, was still always the truth. In hindsight, maybe I knew this day was coming and maybe Galen had been the trigger after all but that knowledge didn't lessen the heartache I felt now. David and I had shared a lifetime together, as friends and as lovers, through our absolute best and sickening worst, and now that had all been ripped out from inside me. I shivered as the first chill of emptiness swept through.

"Figure out what you need to do," he said. "If it's a phase, then get it out of your system. If it's not, then at least we'll know. But I can't be a part of a relationship that's uncertain or that'll lead to resentment. We'll be worse off because of it and neither one of us deserves that."

"David, it's not that I want someone else."

"I think you do. And I also think you're afraid to admit it."

His jaw clenched and he glanced away and I watched him battle the very same emotions I was. Worse, our decades–long relationship had been reduced to little more than awkward words and fast fading hope in less than a day.

"This is a mistake," I told him. "You can't give up on us. I won't let this happen."

David cleared his throat and swung his attention back to me. "Nat's agreed to stay with you in my absence," he said, ignoring what I'd just said. "At least until we figure Logan out."

"David—"

"The cops took him in but I'm not too sure where that's going to lead."

"Wait. What?" My head and heart were still wrapped around David leaving, and I was having trouble keeping up with the abrupt change in topic.

"I ran after Logan but I saw the cops before he did, and I was able to dodge them before they saw me," David said. "But I guess Logan got their radar humming, and they nabbed him and dumped him into their patrol car."

"David, denial and ignorance aren't going to help us any. If you want resentment in our relationship, refusing to face what's ahead of us is a surefire way of giving it a head start. Logan isn't what we should be talking about."

"I don't know how long they'll keep him in custody, but I'm not willing to take any chances with you."

"David, stop!"

"Did you know Logan's a drug dealer?"

"Of course I did—"

"Did you know he's been accused of stalking?"

"What?" I faltered. "No."

"Did you know he was also accused of being an accessory to murder eighteen months ago? My intel told me that the case against him was dismissed and that his file was sealed."

My head felt stuffed up and full of too much information that I couldn't process. "You're throwing too much at me too fast and I can't get a handle on all of it. You have to slow down."

"Then maybe this will help." David dug into his back jeans pocket and pulled out a cell phone. "Logan may have friends in high places who can cover for him, but on his own he's clumsy. He dropped this when I ran after him, and I think you'll be very interested in what you'll find on there."

He handed me the phone and I stared at it, not sure what to think anymore.

"Is it Logan's?" I asked.

"I don't know. It was *on* him."

The downstairs doorbell rang, I heard the front door open, and Nat's voice followed right after. "Avon calling!"

David picked up his duffel bag and started for the door.

"Hello?" Nat shouted.

"Be right down!" David shouted back.

I put the cell on the dresser. "David, please."

"I'm not the one running or hiding this time, Lottie." David's voice and expression softened, giving me a glimpse of the man who loved me but who no longer seemed willing to try. "You are."

He moved in closer, as if he wanted to kiss me, then he changed his mind and left.

I slumped against the wall, numb, unable to move but aware of distant voices, doors opening and closing, footsteps entering and leaving, my mind spinning in neutral as I tried to picture my life ahead without David in it.

I wasn't sure how long I stood there but at some point I became aware of Lori's hands on my shoulders, guiding me to my bed. She settled me down on the covers and fluffed up the pillows behind me.

"Are you okay?" she asked.

I honestly didn't know.

"I'm so sorry, honey." She sat down beside me and pulled me into a tender hug that only a best friend could give. I rested my chin on her shoulder and stared out into space, feeling cut off from the world and from my feelings as well. Nothing seemed to get through. Not her soft sounds of encouragement or the gentle way she stroked my hair. Not even her whispers that promised she'd be there to help me get through.

Only when I was ready did I pull back so I could focus on Lori instead of my own misery.

"You want to talk about it?" she asked, pushing my hair behind an ear.

I shook my head and the hair fell forward.

Lori pulled back a little further to get a better look at me. "Why not? I can be a pretty good therapist, too, you know. Raising three boys definitely gives you insight."

She offered me a smile but I didn't smile back.

"Okay, then. Let's forget about that and move on to something else." Lori stood up, got the remote, turned on the television, and found a comedy. "I know you're going to remind me that this is the worst thing I could offer you, but as your best friend I say it might be one of the best." She dug a bottle of tequila and two shot glasses from her handbag. "You up for a little numbing instead?"

I gave her a weary smile.

"I'll take that as a yes."

"This is all kinds of wrong," I said.

"Please don't go all therapist on me," she said, opening the bottle and pouring two shots. "I don't need to be reminded of how bad it is for a depressed person to drink."

"Actually, I was remembering the last time we numbed. You had a big fight with Nat, came over, drank too much, and ended up shoving David out of my bed so you could sleep here with me. And you didn't give it back to him until three days later."

Lori settled in next to me and handed me a glass. "Just so you know, I intend to do that again."

"Only this time, David's already gone."

Lori's shoulders and expression fell. "I wish there was something I could do to change what happened."

I shrugged. "I know."

"The thing is, I don't really know what happened."

I realized there was no point in holding back from my best friend, and I told her everything that I should have told her from the beginning.

Lori listened, soaking it all in and never once judging my memories, how I felt about Galen, or what I'd done to David. When I finished, she lifted her glass to mine while I worked hard to tough it out and not cry.

"To better times," she toasted.

Amen to that, I thought as I tossed back the tequila, and I rested my head on Lori's shoulder and cried anyway.

Chapter Twenty-Seven

I woke up, unsure of my surroundings until my bedroom, lit by bright morning sun, came into view. My head throbbed, my throat was dry and my tongue felt three times too big for my mouth. I felt edgy and impatient and, in some strange way, trapped.

I stared at the ceiling, trying to put a finger on what unsettled me so much. Part of it had to do with Galen, but the bigger part had to do with David. It wasn't because he'd left, and it wasn't because I wasn't sure when, or if, he would return. It was something else.

It was something darker and more uncertain, and it had to do with Bakari's sword.

I sat up and studied David's empty side of the bed, letting my thoughts and emotions run without restraint. All the hopes, fears, and joys. All the betrayals, promises, and sadness. As they raced through me, reminding me of all I had done right and all I had done wrong in this life and the one before, the true source of what troubled me emerged. I'd been denying it even when David stood at his most adamant, trying to make me see what he saw too well. I had pushed Bakari away because of Kemnebi, and I had pushed David away because of Galen now. But that in itself wasn't the issue. The issue was that I carried unresolved, maybe even long–buried, feelings for Galen.

And David saw them before I did.

I pulled my legs up and rested my chin on my knees. While Galen could help me find closure, I also understood that pursuing that closure could very well come at a price with the man I loved, and denied, through two lifetimes.

Sweeping a hand over David's side of the bed, I felt the cool, soft sheets, drew in the subtle, musky scent of him, and wondered what lay ahead for the both of us. I also wondered if I could change that course of fate with the second chance I'd been given now.

The sound of Lori and Nat's voices from the foyer downstairs broke into my thoughts. They spoke for a while, their tones muffled and subdued, until the front door opened and closed. Then, nothing.

My stomach grumbled, reminding me I should eat, and when I pushed out of bed and stood up, the image of Bakari drawing his sword returned. Then the memory dissolved, but the restless, disturbing feeling remained. It was the same feeling I'd had when I had been brought to the hospital after passing out at Nirvana's bar.

It felt like death.

I shuddered through a chill and now, more than ever, wished that David were here. I pulled his pillow to my chest and as I rested my head on the delicate, Egyptian cotton, another memory moved in.

I was with my servant, Kesi. She was braiding the last few gold tubes into my wig, her head down, her mouth set into an angry line.

"You have not spoken all morning," I told her. "What is on your mind?"

She moved behind me and, while I held a mirror, tugged

the wig onto my head and into place. Hard.

"Does it meet with your pleasure?" she asked in a sharp tone.

I put down the mirror and turned on my stool to face her. "You are angry with me. Why?"

Kesi considered the jar of kohl on a nearby ebony table, looking like she might choose to avoid answering the question and finish my eyes instead, but then her features hardened with bitterness. "You have told Pharaoh about Haji and me."

She said it as if it was a fact. Even though Kesi and I never spoke of that day when I saw her and Haji together in the chamber where I was tutored, I kept their affair to myself. I told no one, not even Bakari.

"I have kept your secret for a long time, Kesi. What makes you think I have told my brother about it?"

"Haji has been sent to the harem in Thebes to tutor the children there."

"When did this happen?"

"You already know when. Do not pretend you do not know anything about this decision."

I was not in the mood to solve riddles, so I stood and closed the space between us. Kesi held her place; chin up, eyes tracking mine.

"We have known one another for many years and you have been my most faithful servant, Kesi, and I would never consider doing such a thing. I have not played any part in what Pharaoh has decided."

Her cheeks burned red with anger and the words rushed forward. "Haji was everything to me, and you had him taken away. It is your fault I will never see him again."

"Did you ever consider that Haji was to be moved to Thebes anyway, because his work as my tutor is complete?"

Kesi lowered her eyes, as if she had not considered the idea until now.

"And, if Pharaoh truly knew about your affair, Kesi, he would have come after you as well. You know that adultery is forbidden. Better to divorce and become involved with another woman or man after, than to do so while living with your husband or wife in the same house."

Kesi glanced away and I wondered if she finally understood the truth in my words. I had done nothing to betray her, and never would.

Then she cocked her head and gave me a sly smile that sent a shiver through my body. "I know that Kemnebi stayed in your chamber last night, Shemei, which not only confirms that you are a liar but a hypocrite and a royal whore as well."

I raised my hand, prepared to slap her, but what she said next turned my blood cold.

"General Bakari is alive and back with Pharaoh now at the Audience Chamber, Shemei. And, as surely as I am standing here, has just received word of your own indiscretion against him. You can thank me for that. Consider it payment for having Haji taken away from me."

I raced out of my chamber and fled to the Audience Chamber, not caring that people were staring at my inappropriate behavior. Once I ascended the granite steps, I stopped to catch my breath and stepped inside. My brother, Pharaoh, was sitting on his throne, a gold kilt on his hips, Crook and Flail in hand, the Double Crown on his head. With the exception of two guards, he was alone.

When he saw me, he motioned for me to come forward and my sandals echoed as I crossed the tiled floor, stepping over images of slain enemies and citizens of other nations subjecting themselves to the King of Egypt. As I approached the throne, another man stepped into view.

Bakari.

I wavered midstride, overwhelmed by his stature and captivated by his striking military regalia and mass. His shoulders had broadened further, his muscles developed with even more definition, and his skin, now shades darker than before, carried a number of fresh scars that still needed time to heal. His hand rested on his gold sword at his hip. His face had hardened, an aftereffect of war I saw on many generals before him, but his eyes still glistened bright green.

His eyes held mine, and I allowed myself to be drawn forward as if under a spell I could not and would not break. I stopped just short of the polished, granite steps leading to the throne, my gaze still one with Bakari. I could find no words to express what I felt but allowed myself precious moments to enjoy the surge of happiness I felt in seeing him again, whole and alive and well. I reached out, wanting to touch him, to feel him, but he tensed and I realized my affection was no longer welcome.

Defeated and deflated, I pulled back and uttered the one thing he probably would never believe but that had to be spoken anyway.

"I am so very sorry."

My brother banged his Crook. "You have brought grief and embarrassment to this family and disappointment to my reign, Shemei," he said. "Although you and General Bakari had no formal marriage contract drawn yet, your sacred bond still existed before the eyes of the gods and of Pharaoh. A bond you plainly and deliberately chose to break. What have you to say?"

Nothing seemed appropriate or sufficient. Still, I could not dismiss this moment and decided to speak the truth because, in the end, it seemed all that mattered.

"My entire life has been shared with Bakari. He is all I have known and all I have ever wanted to know. It was never my intention to hurt anyone. I merely wanted solace because I believed Bakari was dead."

"And you never thought to ask someone if this was true? More so, you never considered how your actions would affect me?"

"No."

My brother studied me in calculating silence. "Why not?"

"I did not think it important because Bakari was my loss, not yours," I said, and I regretted the words as soon as I spoke them.

"General Bakari was in your life because of *me*, Shemei! Do not forget that!" My brother drew in a sharp breath, lifted his chin and considered me with blatant disapproval. After a few moments, he turned and said, "General Bakari?"

Bakari stepped forward. "Your Majesty?"

"I am inclined to dismiss my decision in favor of yours. What have you to say?"

Bakari did not look at me, though he took the time to weigh his thoughts. In those waiting breaths, I recalled the days when Bakari and I grew up, playing in the fields and facing punishment for finding trouble, sharing wine and watching the gods light the night sky while we discovered each other in heart and body. They were times I would not trade for anything or anyone but that I hoped Bakari would consider as he made his decision for our future. I vowed that if he found it in his heart to forgive me, I would never betray or disappoint him again. We shared something unique and what I believed to be a once in a lifetime, and I wanted to live the rest of my lifetime with his.

He squared his shoulders. "I have nothing to say, Your Majesty." He took one step back into place, in deference to his Pharaoh.

His decision came as an unexpected blow and I closed my eyes and choked back a sob. I felt withered and empty, like the dried out, lifeless trees that dotted the edges of the desert. With those few words, Bakari erased my past along with my future, though if I admitted the truth, he did it only because I erased it first.

Very well," my brother said over an exhalation. "Shemei, it is my decision that you will face execution as Re descends tonight. General Bakari?"

"Yes, Your Majesty."

"I order that Shemei will die by your hand and sword."

Pharaoh banged his Crook on his throne and called for the guards. Without any word or even a glance my way, they escorted me from the Audience Chamber. I followed them with blind trust because I did not know in which direction I walked. My eyes remained fixed on Bakari until the Chamber doors closed after me, cutting my life from his.

The memory shut down and I launched from the bed as realization kicked in.

"Oh my God," I said, grabbing a fresh tee and shorts from the dresser. "It's happening all over again."

I hadn't seen it until now. I had betrayed Bakari and lost him when he discovered my duplicity, and I now faced losing David, too, under very similar circumstances. Only this time, *this time*, I could change the course of fate before it was too late. David may have been Bakari back then but he wasn't Bakari now, and that was the key difference. We may have shared a past life and brought lessons to learn into this one, but we were also different people now, facing different choices.

And I intended to use those new choices to make things right.

I freshened up, jumped into my clothes, tugged on a pair of Keds and flew down the stairs to the kitchen. Nat was slouched in David's chair at the kitchen table, reading the news on David's tablet, and drinking coffee from David's mug.

"Where is David?" I asked.

Nat lowered the tablet and looked at me. "Good morning to you, too."

"I need to talk to David. Where is he?"

Nat considered me for a few cautious seconds before putting down the tablet. "What's going on? Are you okay?"

"I'll be better once I explain everything to David."

I found my cell phone plugged into the charger on the kitchen desk, snagged it and dialed. The call went into David's voicemail. I left a message saying that it was important and I needed to talk to him right away. Then I fished through the desk drawer for my Jeep's keys. Nat grabbed my hand before I found them.

"What are you doing, Lottie?"

"I'm going to find David."

"He doesn't want to see you right now."

I shoved at Nat's massive chest, wanting him out of the way. "I'll change his mind."

I had to. I had to make things right again and there was only one way to do it.

"So what are you gonna do? Drive around all his haunts, looking for him?"

"If I have to. But it would be easier if you just tell me where he is."

"That's not gonna happen." Nat placed his hands on either side of me, cornering me against the granite countertop. "My best friend said he wanted time alone and asked me to watch his girl, and I'm gonna do that. You understand what that means?"

"Step aside, Nat."

"You're a friend, Lottie, but you're not David. I won't betray him like you betrayed him."

"You have no idea what's going on."

"I know more than you think I do."

I wondered what David had told him and decided it didn't matter. "Your loyalty may be to David," I told him, "but remember that you're going to have to answer to David when he discovers you're the reason he and I couldn't make things right between us."

Nat pulled back, but only slightly. Then his cell phone rang and, after considering me a little while longer, backed away and answered. For a brief moment, I wondered if David was on the other end of the line. When Nat disconnected, he looked at me with a seriousness I'd never seen in him before.

"Bad news, Lottie."

I held steady, waiting.

"I got intel on the hair from that envelope you got last week," Nat said. "Wasn't yours."

"But it looked like mine."

He shook his head and clipped the phone to his waist. "Dyed. Came from a long–haired blonde."

I knew only one person who had long blonde hair. "Mrs. Reynolds."

"Who's Mrs. Reynolds?"

I didn't answer and darted out of the kitchen instead, remembering Logan's phone that David had given me yesterday and that I'd left upstairs when Lori and I knocked back the tequila. "Be right back," I called out, and I took off for my bedroom.

Nat followed, peppering me with questions. "What are you doing? What's going on? Whose phone is that?"

I ignored him and started cycling through the text history. In there, I found the texts I received while I waited for Paul in the Amrose parking lot the other day.

"Lottie, tell me what's going on."

"I'm not exactly sure."

The front doorbell rang and I told Nat to answer it. While he headed downstairs, I cycled through the call history next. There, I found the call made to my house last Friday by the man who knew about my dream, along with dozens of others to a phone number I didn't know. Curious, I pressed redial.

While I waited for someone to answer, I heard two sets of footsteps ascend the stairs and head toward my bedroom.

A woman picked up the phone and said, "Paul? Is that

222 | TERRI HERMAN-PONCE

you?"

I stilled when I realized it was Mrs. Reynolds.

"Say something, Paul. I don't like secrets or being lied to."

Nat's voice broke into my confused silence. "You got company, Lottie."

I looked up and discovered Paul standing next to him.

Chapter Twenty-Eight

I disconnected the call and took a step back, watching Paul with caution.

"Why are you here?" I asked.

His face showed bewilderment at the question, then apprehension when he saw the cell phone in my hand.

I held it up. "Explain this."

"It's a cell phone. It's used to make phone calls."

"That's not what I meant and you know it. Try again."

Paul hesitated.

"It's all here on this phone," I said. "The texts and the calls you made to me. Why did you do it?"

"I haven't done anything."

Nat moved in beside me. "What's going on?"

Paul's eyes flicked to Nat then settled back on me. "I came here to apologize for what happened yesterday."

I looked at Nat. "This is Paul's phone. It's filled with phone calls made to Mrs. Reynolds, and incriminating texts and calls made to me. David found it on Logan yesterday, and I suspect that's why Logan's been trying to meet with me. He discovered what I needed to know."

"The calls we've been investigating?" he asked.

"Yes." I looked back at Paul. "Did you send the hair, too?"

"What hair?" Paul asked. "Lottie, you're not making any sense and you're agitated." He turned to Nat. "She needs to be sedated."

"He's lying," I told Nat.

"You've seen her behavior lately, haven't you?" Paul asked. "Lottie has been experiencing episodes that have no basis in reality and these episodes seem to be getting worse. She needs attention. Promptly."

Paul took a step closer and I stood firm. "You're not denying anything. In fact, I'd say that your evasiveness over my accusations only shows just how guilty you are."

For one brief moment I saw Paul's expression soften, giving me a glimpse of the man I thought I knew. I thought about what Mrs. Reynolds said on the phone, about her not liking his secrets, and I wondered what other secrets Paul kept hidden from me, too. Then his features hardened and the Paul I knew faded away.

"We were best friends for years, Paul," I said. "I've confided in you and you in me. Why do this? Was it because I chose David instead of you?"

"Help me restrain her," Paul said to Nat. "And I'll get her hospitalized and under observation."

Nat's gaze volleyed between the two of us.

"Was it because I never gave us a chance?" I asked.

Paul pressed his lips together.

"I'm sorry that things didn't work out for us, and I'm sorry I hurt you, Paul. You have to know I never intended to cause you any pain."

Paul remained silent but there was heaviness in his silence that didn't sit well, and I knew that wasn't all of it. There had to be more at stake here. But what? I remembered the photo of his niece, Deborah, which Paul kept in its prideful place on the shelf in his office, where everyone could see it, and knew I had the bigger answer.

"Was it because of what happened to Deborah?"

Paul flinched and I knew I had him.

"Was it?" When Paul didn't respond, I asked, "Was it because Deborah was like the daughter you never had?"

Paul swallowed and a small bead of sweat rolled down the side of his face.

"Was it because she was depressed and you couldn't help her?"

His jaw clenched.

"Or was it because I couldn't help her either? Are you blaming me for her death?"

"It *was* your fault!" Paul fired back. "You found another psychiatrist and had him prescribe a medication you knew carried increased risk of suicide in teenagers. And you did nothing about it. She had her whole life ahead of her, and you didn't look for the signs, and by the time we realized what was going on it was too late!"

"And you're going to make me pay for it."

"You deserve it," Paul grated, then his tone turned apologetic. "That didn't come out the way I meant, Lottie."

"I think it did."

Nat tugged the phone from his waist.

"Put that down," Paul said. "There's no need to call for help. I can take care of her. She needs psychiatric help at a proper facility. She needs a psychiatrist who can look after her."

Paul moved for me and Nat stepped in between. "I'll call whoever I think I need, buddy. The lady wants answers," he said. "I suggest you give them to her."

Paul snagged the cell from my hand.

"Call David," I told Nat. "Now."

Chapter Twenty-Nine

Nat tackled Paul, knocking the cell phone from his hand. It skittered across the tile floor and I raced to pick it up. I heard a body slam against a wall and the sound of fist on bone, followed by heavy breathing and then silence. When I turned around, Nat was hefting an unconscious Paul into a seated position against a wall. Paul had a giant welt on his cheek and a split lip.

"Is he going to be okay?" I asked.

"Don't worry about this jerk–wad." Nat turned to me. "You got any rope or twine so I can tie him up before he comes around? He won't be out forever."

Paul looked peaceful and composed and more like the man I used to know. Or thought I knew. In hindsight, it all seemed so obvious now—what Paul had done and why he'd done it— and the truth hurt. I'd trusted him and never saw the betrayal coming. I didn't even see his need for revenge.

"The rope's in the garage," I said.

Nat went to find the rope and I called David again, only to leave another message. As soon as I hung up, Nat returned and my cell phone rang.

Logan didn't wait for my hello. "I need your help, Doctor Morgan."

He sounded distressed and I wasn't sure what to make of it. It wasn't the first time he'd tried playing games with me, and I knew there was no reason it would be different now.

"Where are you?" I asked, watching Nat tie up Paul.

"Home and I need you to come over. Something's going down with my mother."

"Are you in danger? Do you need me to call the police?"

"No." Logan's voice dropped. "She's acting weird. She's pacing around, mumbling shit to herself, saying stuff about this guy, Paul, that she's been dating, and saying stuff about you, too. She looks all wired, like she's whacked out or something, and keeps saying she has to get to you. I don't get what's happening."

I glanced at Paul on the floor, bound by his hands and feet. Nat was searching through his wallet and personal phone.

"Is she coherent?" I asked.

"Sorta. It started when we got home, after she posted my bail with the cops. She didn't say nothing in the car, but she got a phone call from Paul a couple of minutes ago and something got her spooked."

I intended to head over and evaluate the situation firsthand but remembered the dozens of times Logan had told stories before. Then I heard his mother in the background, calling out Paul's name, and knew he was telling the truth. Paul had lied to me and withheld from me, and I knew there was more to him that I had to find out. And Logan and Mrs. Reynolds could complete the picture.

"Okay," I said. "Give me your address and I'll head over right now."

I shoved Paul's cell phone in one back pocket and my own in the other, and returned to the kitchen for my keys. Nat followed and grabbed my hand.

"Wait for David first," he said.

"I can't. Logan needs me. You're done here and I have the evidence that proves it's been Paul all along." I patted my back pocket where I had stashed the phone.

"Lottie, I'm only gonna say this once."

"Consider it said. I'll see you later."

Nat cursed but didn't follow, and I made it to Mrs. Reynolds's driveway in Huntington Bay in less than thirty minutes. Well tended with huge trees and rolling hills, the mansion looked like something from a magazine cover. I sat in the Jeep, idling and wondering how I would handle the meeting. At the first sign of trouble, I decided I was calling the police.

I cut the engine, walked up the long, cobblestone driveway to the front entrance, and rang the doorbell, unsure of what to expect on the other side. One of the massive wood, double doors swung open and Logan peered out at me from the inside. A chandelier the size of a small car hung over a foyer as big as my entire first floor.

"Where is she?" I asked.

"In the living room."

"Does she know I'm coming?"

Logan shook his head.

I stepped over the threshold, heard Mrs. Reynolds call out Paul's name again, and followed the direction of her voice with Logan close behind. My Keds squeaked across the inlaid, undoubtedly imported wood floor.

"My mother's gonna try and play you," Logan whispered as we entered a living room that had two fireplaces and was decorated with furniture and art that I guessed totaled more

230 | TERRI HERMAN-PONCE

than my annual salary.

Mrs. Reynolds was sitting on a raw silk wing chair reading *Vogue* magazine near the larger fireplace. "Paul? Where have you been?" She looked up from her magazine at Logan and then to me, rose from her chair, smoothed her black dress, and gave me a cordial smile.

"Doctor Morgan, what a pleasant surprise. What brings you here this afternoon?"

Logan gave me another warning look and took a position near a tapestry sofa. I headed for the wing chair beside his mother.

"Logan called me because he said you were asking for me," I said. "I apologize that I showed up unannounced. I hope you don't mind."

Mrs. Reynolds's mouth thinned and an unspoken message passed between her and her son. Then Logan told her to go to hell. She apologized to me on his behalf and motioned to the vacant chair next to her.

"You'll have to excuse Logan today, Doctor Morgan. He's been a little under the weather lately."

"Is everything all right?" I asked, taking a seat.

She gave me a forced smile and glanced at Logan, another silent look passing between them. "I suppose I should have called you at the office or made a more formal appointment, but it isn't often that Logan looks after me. The fact that he called you today and that you responded so quickly means a lot to me."

Logan rolled his eyes.

Mrs. Reynolds sighed.

"What happened?" I asked.

She appeared uncertain at first.

"It's alright, Mrs. Reynolds. I only want to help. We don't have to talk about anything in particular, right now, if you don't want to. But I *am* concerned."

She tossed the magazine to the thick, carpeted floor. "Well, I've been having trouble with a man I've been dating at the same time I was having trouble with Logan." She glanced at him again. "When Logan left a note saying he wanted to leave, this man threatened to do the same, and I fell apart. I couldn't handle it, and then it seemed we might be patching things up and…" She cast her eyes downward in embarrassment, and after several moments of reflection looked back up. "I am so very sorry for lying to you when we met in your office, Doctor Morgan. I was just trying to cope. It was wrong of me and I realize that, but I was simply reacting to my situation."

"I can understand that. It's a very normal response for someone under extreme stress."

I studied her for signs of stress now, along with the erratic behavior Logan warned me about earlier. None of that seemed present. In fact, Mrs. Reynolds appeared companionable and pleasant. On the surface I knew she wasn't telling the entire truth, but that was expected with clients sometimes. Sometimes, it just took them a little longer to feel comfortable enough with their therapist to openly share their feelings.

"Where are my manners?" Mrs. Reynolds stood. "Can I get you something?"

"It's not necessary."

"It's fine, Doctor Morgan. I truly would like to talk with you, but it is time for my early afternoon tea. I have a cup every day after lunch. Would you care to join me? I believe my maid has arranged a lovely green blend in the kitchen, and I would be more than happy to bring you some."

It was the first ordinary thing someone had asked me to do in days and, not wanting to appear ungrateful, I agreed.

When she left the living room I turned to Logan. "Your mother doesn't seem 'spooked.' In fact, she seems in a very pleasant mood."

Logan glanced toward the doorway and listened to the noises coming from the kitchen. "I swear something's wrong."

"What do you think is wrong?"

"She wasn't like this before you came. She was freaking, big time, saying stuff about how the only way she could resolve anything was if she got to you before Paul did. Do you know this guy, Doctor Morgan? Coz my mother made it sound like you did."

Mrs. Reynolds returned with a gold tray laden with fine china, a sugar bowl, two filled cups and a small teapot. She handed me a cup and offered sugar, which I declined. When she settled into her chair, she mixed sugar into her own tea and sipped. I did the same. It was hot and tasted like berries.

"I am grateful we were finally able to come together," she said, placing her tea on a nearby table. "I've been considering family counseling for a while now."

"To be honest, Mrs. Reynolds—"

"Please, call me Casey."

"Logan said you were upset before I got here, Casey, and that's the primary reason I came today. Did something happen?"

"Logan has a tendency to exaggerate. I was watching a

television program, one of those reality shows, and I guess I got a little passionate about it."

I glanced at Logan, waiting for a reaction, but none came.

"I'd like to provide family counseling for you both," I said, "but, as I mentioned before, I also want to make sure that everything is okay. I'd also like to use this time to better understand your relationship with Logan, if you're open to that."

"That would be nice."

I placed my half–empty cup on a nearby table and the room swayed as I sat up. I braced myself until the dizziness passed and tried listening to what Casey was saying but was having difficulty concentrating on her words. I felt memories tug at me again, trying to pull me back in time, and I wondered if this was what Galen meant when he said his own regression hadn't been easy.

The dizziness passed and Casey's voice eased back in. "I would like to talk about Paul first, if you don't mind." She placed her empty cup beside mine. "He's the gentleman I've been dating and, well, Logan hasn't exactly warmed up to him. I believe he is one of the primary reasons there's a rift between me and my son."

"You're so full of shit," Logan said. "We had a *rift* before Paul came around." He looked at me. "In case you didn't figure it out, Paul's also my mother's psychiatrist."

My mouth went dry as I received confirmation that Paul had lied to me about his relationship with Casey.

"Have you been seeing Paul for a while?" I asked.

"About two months." Casey refilled her tea and looked at me through the steam that curled up from the cup as she drank.

"I know you had a relationship with him, too. Paul told me about it."

A burning sensation tore through my stomach and I swallowed over my growing distress. "Did you know that a sexual relationship between a psychiatrist and patient is unethical and grounds for suspension or revocation of license?"

Casey put her cup and saucer down again. "Yes, and that's why I came to you initially for help."

I thought back to the excuse she'd used, about Logan committing suicide, when she first contacted me a few days ago. "Why lie about it?" I asked.

"Told you that already," Logan said. "She was trying to get your attention."

Casey sighed. "Paul started threatening me, saying he wanted to end the relationship, and I was afraid he might get abusive and I didn't know what to do about it."

"Did he get physical with you?"

"No, but I was worried that he might. And that's why I lied to get your attention, but it was only because I knew he had an affair with you and I hoped you would help me because you'd known him so intimately. For obvious reasons, I couldn't come right out and say what I needed from you because I couldn't risk Paul losing his ability to practice psychiatry."

She swallowed and her features softened with tenderness and affection. It was then I realized Casey was in love with Paul.

"Given that Paul has threatened you, Casey, I'd like to discuss him in more detail. I think there are some things you need to know." I dug into my back pocket and fumbled for his cell phone. I blinked several times, trying to fight double vision and another bout of dizziness, and finally tugged it free. "This is important to me because he's been threatening *me*, and he's been using his cell phone to do it."

Logan moved in to get a better look and took the phone from my hands. "That's not Paul's cell. That's the phone David snagged from me yesterday before the cops took me in. It belongs to my mother."

The burning sensation crawled up from my stomach into my throat. "I don't understand."

I waited for an explanation but was overcome by a feverish sweat that left my skin wet and clammy. I blinked through a haze that distorted Casey's features, splitting her into two women and then three. She was looking at me. I glanced at the teacups and saw six of them, and tasted the remnants of the green tea in my mouth along with a subtle bitterness I didn't notice before.

I clutched my stomach, moaning over pain that tore through my abdomen, and fell to the floor.

"I need…help."

"Doctor Morgan?" Logan raced to my side and tried helping me sit up but my arms and legs started convulsing, and I couldn't make the convulsions stop.

Casey shoved him away.

I peered up at her, rolled over, and threw up.

Logan turned on his mother. "What the hell did you do to her?"

"I gave her what she deserved." Casey squatted down next to me, smiling now. "How was the tea, Shemei? Does it meet with your pleasure?"

I remembered the voice—the woman—and all the years she had asked me that very question. How she soothed me when I was sick, and encouraged me when I was sad. How she sounded pleased when my makeup was exceptionally applied and my sheer linen sheaths were perfectly styled. I remembered her teaching me the ways of satisfying a man, and her excitement when she discovered I had given myself to Bakari—and used what she'd taught me to please him.

I remembered her anger when she thought I'd told Pharaoh about her affair with Haji, and her disdain the day she discovered my infidelity to Bakari. And I remembered her smile of triumph when Pharaoh, embarrassed by my transgression before his people, allies and enemies, ordered my execution by Bakari's sword.

I rolled over and faced Casey again. Pain tore through my belly once more.

"Yes, Shemei, it is me," she said, brushing my hair from my cheek. "And I must say, I'm so disappointed in you. You have betrayed so many men in your lifetimes." Casey's eyes softened and I sensed the love she once felt for me so long ago. "I understand you've been experiencing your own regression very recently. Paul helped me through mine when we met two months ago. Isn't it amazing how our lives have come full circle?"

My body convulsed again and a tingling sensation swept through my legs and arms. Then my limbs fell limp and numb. I looked up at Logan. "Call…for help."

Casey stroked my cheek. "You look so much like Shemei, it's truly amazing."

Behind Casey, Logan started moving away from us.

"Please," I rasped over a ragged breath. "Call. Help."

"I miss those days, don't you?" Casey asked.

I wanted to shake my head and tell her no. I wanted what I had now. What was so precious to me and that I might never get back, for a second time.

"But I don't miss all of them," she said. "You found out about my relationship with Haji and told Pharaoh."

I didn't tell him.

"You betrayed me in a past life, and you have betrayed Paul in this one."

No.

Logan stood at the doorway to the foyer now, shifting on his feet.

Tears filled Casey's eyes. "I love Paul, as much now as I did when he tutored you." She kept stroking my cheek. My hair. "But he loved you instead. You never knew that Haji loved you, did you?"

No.

"Or that Paul still loves you now?"

I searched for Logan. He wasn't there.

"You betrayed me, and then slept with Kemnebi even when you weren't sure what had really happened to Bakari."

It was a mistake.

"Then you told Pharaoh about Haji and had him taken from me." Casey's tears fell to my face. "It was because of you that I lost him. And so I told Pharaoh about you and Kemnebi. I had to make sure that you felt the same pain and loss that I did."

I felt it. More than you realize.

"That is why I'm going to get you out of the way now.

Only then can Paul truly be mine."

Logan. Please. Where are you?

"You won't take him from me again, Shemei."

Casey grabbed a poker from the fireplace and raised it overhead, and I saw it all. Swimming in the river. Drinking stolen wine. Time spent alone with Bakari, learning of love near the Nile beneath a brilliant starry sky. The heat and passion in Kemnebi's body and how it perfectly molded to mine. The pain I'd caused Bakari when he found out what I'd done once Kesi told Pharaoh. The tears that ran down his cheeks when Pharaoh ordered my death, and the glint of his sword angling down toward me.

Kemnebi, pleading for my life and demanding that Bakari should take his instead of mine.

And Bakari's last words to me.

I am yours and you are mine. For always. Forgive me, as I have forgiven you.

Casey aimed the poker and swung down.

I closed my eyes and left this life.

Forgiven.

Chapter Thirty

Someone was whispering my name.

I felt fingertips brush the hair from my face, coaxing me back. My eyes fluttered open and I discovered David sitting beside me. His green eyes were filled with concern but his smile was relieved and tender.

"How are you feeling?" he asked.

"Okay, I think." I took the time to ground myself and figure out where I was. "Emergency room?" I asked over a raspy throat.

David nodded and handed over a small cup of water that I downed in three gulps.

"How long?" I asked.

"You've been in and out of sleep since you got here fourteen hours ago." David took the empty cup and set it off to the side. Then he swept a gentle hand over my hair again. "Do you remember anything?"

I nodded, remembering too much, and shot up in bed, realizing what I didn't. "Where is Logan's mother? And Logan? And how did I get here?"

David hushed me and coaxed me back into the pillows. A monitor beside the bed beeped in time with my heart and an intravenous line was hooked up to my left arm. "Take a few minutes first, okay? Moving too fast isn't a good idea right now."

"David," I persisted, "please tell me what happened."

He frowned but gave in. "After I got your call, I raced back home. Nat told me what had happened between you and Paul and that you went to Logan's house after he phoned you. I followed you there."

"Why?"

"After I packed and left the house, I started poking around the PROs database for information on Paul and Mrs. Reynolds. She popped up in the system with a long history of drug–related charges, mostly abuse related to antidepressants. And guess who the prescriber was."

"Paul?"

David nodded. "I had a gut feeling about her and when Nat said that Logan was having an issue with her, I started doing the math. That's why I followed."

"And that's where you found me?"

He nodded again. "I called an ambulance when I found you unconscious and followed you to the emergency room. The doctor said you had elevated levels of bupropion in your blood."

"Bupropion? That's an antidepressant."

"Yeah, that's what they told me. They said you were lucky because you could have overdosed, but the hospital staff monitored you through the night and said you'll be fine. They're going to discharge you sometime today."

I looked at the wall clock. It was almost six in the morning.

"Casey Reynolds tried to kill me," I said.

"Yes. And she almost succeeded."

"Where is she now?"

David stared at me for several drawn out seconds. "Dead."

I didn't have to ask how she died. The resolute look in his eyes gave me the answer.

"You saved my life," I whispered.

David caressed my cheek, his warm fingertips lingering there as if he still needed to be reminded that I had survived.

"What happened to Logan?" I asked. "And Paul?"

"Logan disappeared. There was no sign of him when I got to his house, but if the authorities find him he'll be dealt with."

I remembered the note he left for his mother, about wanting to leave home and not wanting to be found. Sadly, it looked like Logan had gotten his wish.

"Paul was taken in by the cops. He'll be brought up on charges. I'm sure of it."

"I've failed again," I said. "First with Deborah, now with Logan and his mother."

"You can't save everyone, Lottie."

But how I wished I could.

David took my hand and I thought about the things I'd learned recently. That past lives really did exist. That, for some reason, certain people returned to a new life so that they could continue learning. To keep going on a specific journey until they were ready to move on.

I wondered what journey was intended for me.

"I think Paul wanted retribution for my choosing you over him," I said. "At first, I thought he was only trying to get back at me for Deborah's death, but Casey said he was still in love with me even though he was in a relationship with her. I think Paul used her on many levels, David, to try and ruin me. She loved him and he took advantage."

David stroked a thumb over my fingers. "Love is a powerful motivator, Lottie. It'll drive people to do some really crazy things."

"Like stalking."

David gave me a questioning look.

"Casey had been stalking me. I'm sure of it now."

"You think Paul put her up to it?"

I shrugged. "I have no idea. Logan made it sound like Casey was unstable, and she probably was, which means she was capable of doing a lot more than I gave her credit for. The fact that she abused antidepressants certainly didn't help."

"I'm sorry you had to go through all of this," David said.

I thought about the final moments I experienced as Shemei, and wondered why Kemnebi offered his life in exchange for mine. I remembered Bakari's forgiveness in the end and, in that moment, understood David in a way I'd never understood him before.

With a sigh, I understood exactly who Galen was, too.

"So, you want to tell me what happened to you?" David asked. "The version you're not going to tell the cops?"

It was a question I was expecting that I knew I couldn't answer. I looked at David and my heart sank as all the years we'd shared together slipped away. All the trust, all the joy, all the heartache and love, all the effort we made to keep our relationship alive and honest, disintegrated like the fragile pages of a centuries–old book.

I shook my head, feeling disappointment and sadness settle inside my heavy heart.

"I can't, David. I just don't think you'll understand."

Chapter Thirty-One

Officer Jim McKarren took my statement while David and Officer Llewellyn listened. I kept my answers simple and to the point, and shortly after one o'clock, when they left the hospital to continue their investigation, I was discharged.

David drove me home in his SUV but we didn't speak along the way. Despite his outer appearance of calm, I knew he felt restless on the inside. And I did, too. It felt as if a huge chasm had surfaced between us, distant and gaping and that would never close unless one of us made the first move to heal it.

Neither of us tried.

I closed my eyes and thought about how much had changed in the past week. My life felt surreal now, and nothing like it used to be. I thought about how much David didn't, or couldn't, understand about my past, and I wanted to believe that his inability to accept that part of me was the reason for the rift between us. But I couldn't lie to myself any longer. I'd learned something important about Kemnebi and me before I'd almost died at Casey's house, and it needed to be addressed. If it wasn't, I didn't think I'd ever fully understand or appreciate who I was right now.

We pulled into the garage and David killed the engine. I noticed that someone had already brought my Jeep back home.

"David," I said, stopping him before he got out of the

SUV. "There's something I need to take care of."

He pulled back into his seat and appraised me. "And that means what, exactly?" he asked, though I had a strong suspicion he already knew the answer.

"It's something I need to do alone."

His jaw clenched and he nodded, but with little enthusiasm. "We have to talk, Lottie."

"I know." But that wasn't going to happen now.

I went inside and found my handbag and the Jeep's keys next to it. David tugged my cell phone from his back jeans pocket and handed it over without a word. I took it and returned to the garage, admitting that I'd spent too many years keeping him at emotional arm's length, realizing that I'd never really let him completely into my heart and asking for far too much from him without giving the same in return. David had put up a good fight for us, even after Galen entered the picture. Now it seemed the fight in him had died. If it hadn't, maybe he wouldn't have been so willing to let me go.

For the second time in days I ended up on Galen's doorstep. I rang the bell with as much reservation as I felt the first time though for very different reasons. This time, I understood exactly what we were to each other.

Galen answered the door and our gazes locked and held. "You have seen what you needed to see," he said.

I nodded. "Can I talk to you?"

He motioned that I should step inside.

We both entered the living area and I stood near the sofa, not because I needed physical distance from Galen but because I now saw his condo's décor with new appreciation. The framed Egyptian artwork and faience pottery. The beveled mirrors edged with coral and lapis and ebony.

The vase filled with fresh blue lotus flowers.

Those furnishings were no longer a visual link to my past but to an emotional one instead.

I turned to him and asked the one question that burned inside my brain. The one I didn't ask thousands of years ago when Kemnebi, kneeling before Bakari, offered his life for mine.

"Why?"

For a moment Galen looked confused, then he smiled and regarded me with equally new appreciation. "That has been the question that has concerned you throughout most of your regression, wouldn't you say?"

"Yes," I said, "but this time I ask it because, right now, there's only one answer I'm looking for."

"Is it important for you to know that answer?"

I moved in closer so that we stood only inches apart. I felt his warmth. Sensed his tranquility and calm. Smelled the rich, spiced scent that I recognized as the two of us. I inhaled and let the scent settle deep inside me, where it felt like it belonged.

"Yes, it's important," I finally said, unable to hide the huskiness in my voice. "I need to know because this is important to me, Galen. Did Bakari kill me like he had been ordered to do? Or did something else happen that I can't see?"

Galen's gaze traced my face, moved lower, and then returned to hold mine. His mouth softened with a wistfulness I hadn't seen in him before. "I wish I could tell you but I can't."

"But I need to know, Galen. I remember Bakari forgiving me in the end but I still remember his sword sweeping down to strike me. Not you, even when you bartered for my life. *Me*."

He cupped my face in his hands. "What Bakari did that night, because of what you and I had done together, changed our lives forever. That is all I can and will say. You must find your own truth on this, Shemei. You must let the memory play out for you on its own, when the time is right."

"But when will that be? Tomorrow? Next week? In five years?"

"If it is to happen, it will take however long it needs to take."

"But you know."

"Yes."

In my heart I knew that whatever Bakari had done that night, and the days and nights leading up to it since he discovered my infidelity, explained a lot of who David was now. On a subconscious level, David must have known that he'd done something to me so long ago. Something he never recovered from, that he refused to see, and that made him overly protective of me now. Maybe it was his inability to forgive me until it was too late. Maybe it was my believing Kemnebi's lie too easily that Bakari had died, just so I could sleep with him. Maybe it was something else that I still didn't know. Whatever it was, it had impacted him. Just as it had impacted me.

"You know," Galen said, "I think that Bakari's actions that night may be the very reason that Bellotti cannot come to terms with what you have learned about yourself. I believe he, on a subconscious level, still carries guilt even after thousands of years have passed and he simply cannot face it."

"I also believe that's why David won't consent to your joining his team," I added. "I think he's transferred that guilt onto you as suspicion and mistrust."

I took the time to more deeply consider the implications of what that meant. And there were many. So much of what we'd done as Shemei, Bakari, and Kemnebi impacted our decisions now. Even our relationships and thoughts and emotions. It was as if unfinished business still lingered, waiting and needing to be resolved.

"But this all leads me back to the one question you refuse to answer, Galen. I heard your appeal in those moments before I was supposed to die. Why did you trade your soul for mine?"

"I did not trade my soul, Shemei."

"But I heard what you said. You bargained for my life."

"No." Galen shook his head and his mouth eased up into a knowing smile. "I bargained for your afterlife. Your *second* life."

I stopped breathing, not completely understanding.

"You are important to me, Shemei. You always have been. It is as simple as that."

"But our relationship was physical, Galen," I said. "Nothing more."

"Was it? Can you look back and truly believe that?"

I couldn't. I wanted to, as much for my sake as David's, but couldn't. Galen and I were as bound as Kemnebi and Shemei had been, and in a way I might never fully appreciate.

"Who knows why any of us received a second chance, Shemei. Yet we all managed to get it, didn't we?"

Galen's voice, so deep and rich and lilting, moved through me like honeyed wine, warming my blood and soothing my soul. I felt drawn to him, as I had always been drawn to him, and the long dormant fire from a lifetime past, the one I'd worked so hard to control, flickered and ignited.

I slipped out from under his hold and distanced myself from his consuming touch. It was too much too fast, and the harder I tried ignoring the emotional grasp Galen had on me, the stronger it intensified. Eventually, something was going to give and any decision I made, either way, was going to have considerable consequences.

"You know that we have a connection," Galen went on. "It is there and it is not something we can deny."

I remembered the time we spent together and the way he made me feel. I remembered the forbidden things we had done and the short–sighted decision I'd made, the lie I'd told myself, to do it.

"It was one night, Galen. Only one. That's not something I'd label as a connection."

"And yet you came to me. You chose me."

"And you lied to me."

"Yes. I did." Galen leaned against the sofa beside me and sighed. "It is a regret I live with every day. But yet, you chose to believe that lie. And for a very specific reason."

He was right. There was no point in denying it.

"So now it is my turn to ask." Galen cupped my chin again. "Why?"

I thought of every reason I used to justify my choice that night. Thought of all the years I knew Bakari and the few short months I knew Kemnebi. I thought of how contented and complete Bakari made me feel, and how Kemnebi lit a fire inside me.

"It's as if we are two parts of a whole," I said. "It's as if I've known you forever, and yet I know you so very little."

"And so here you are, faced with another decision similar to the one you made before, Shemei."

"I'm not Shemei, Galen."

His thumb caressed my bottom lip. "You are more Shemei than you realize."

"This situation is different. Or rather, it can be different. We are different people living in a different time."

"With a shared past. And if you truly believe that we are so different, then perhaps you have not been looking hard enough." Galen rested his hands on my shoulders. "Like before, you have your choices of either doing or not doing. Things happened for a reason, and will happen again for a reason."

"Maybe."

"Definitely."

I brushed my hair from my face and swept my hands over my eyes. I was so tired. Tired of thinking, tired of analyzing, tired of trying too hard to find answers for decisions I couldn't make.

Galen pressed in closer. "We do not remember days, Shemei, we remember moments, and the richness of life lies in memories we have forgotten."

"I can't forget my past, Galen. Not now."

"I am not asking you to." He pulled me to him. "I instead ask you to look to your future. A new and different one."

He kissed me then, and in his arms I found my answer.

Chapter Thirty-Two

It was long past dinnertime when I pulled up my driveway and into the garage. David's SUV was parked inside and uncertainty surged through me at the sight of it. He was still home and that meant there was no turning back now.

After cutting the engine, I walked through the laundry room and kitchen, not sure what to expect when I told David what needed to be said. We'd been through a lot over the years but even more during the past week, and though our relationship was already hanging by a thin, fragile thread, this had to be done. The big question was how he would handle my news.

I dropped my keys on the desk next to David's and, seeing an empty den and kitchen, decided to head upstairs to find him. Each step I took felt heavy and tentative. I had no idea what would greet me once I found him.

I stopped just outside our bedroom and took a few moments to collect my thoughts. I reminded myself that David and I relied on honesty since we'd moved in together, and there was no reason for that honesty to have changed now. If he would open his mind and just listen, maybe that would be enough. In my heart, I hoped and prayed that it was.

With one final deep breath, I stepped over the threshold and found David sitting on the edge of our bed, hands clasped, head down. He looked up when I walked in and held me with a sharp, insightful gaze. The bags under his eyes confirmed his fatigue and the set of his jaw showed that he wasn't in the mood for games. In his drawn features, I saw the stress he was trying hard to hide.

"Have a minute?" I asked him. "I need to talk to you."

He paused, too long for my comfort, and patted the spot on the bed beside him.

He didn't look at me as I sat down, nor did he touch me. He kept a safe distance, for emotional protection I realized, and said nothing. He was giving me the opportunity to say it all, and maybe decide it all as well.

"I realized some very important things today, David." I studied his resolute profile and his unblinking eyes and the way he kept staring ahead, as if constructing an invisible wall between us. "And there will be a time, a more appropriate time, to explain it all to you, but now isn't it."

He didn't react.

I took it as a signal to keep going.

"You need to know that I didn't sleep with Galen."

He blinked, once.

"I'm attracted to him. I won't lie to you about that. But you're my life. You always have been and always will be."

David remained silent and still, and I started wondering if my reconciliation was too little too late.

"I went to his house this afternoon to talk," I added, "and Galen said some things that resonated with me."

And so here you are, faced with another decision similar to the one you made before.

I instead ask you to look to your future. A new and different one.

"I understand better now why I've been so distant with you," I said. "And why I've avoided marriage. Someday, when we're both ready, I'll tell you the whole story. Just know that I never intended to hurt you. I was running away from something wonderful simply because I was scared, and it was Galen who helped me understand why."

David straightened. "I've always known you were scared of marriage, Lottie. This isn't news to me."

His blunt words, and the impatience behind them, pushed me into the offensive. If I was going to make this right, I had only one shot and only one time to do it.

"True," I said, "but the reasons for my fear are because of a decision I made a long time ago."

He made a face that said he wasn't completely convinced. "Let me guess. Your memories?"

"I understand your irritation, David. I've demanded a lot from you recently and, if the situation was reversed, I'm sure I would have acted on the same disbelief and distrust that you did." I paused, recognizing the precious gift David had given me throughout my regression. "You gave me the opportunity to figure out my life with Galen as a guide, and the freedom to find what I needed to find. I'm not sure I would have been able to do the same for you, which probably doesn't say a whole lot for who I am as a person. What I'm trying to say is, I love you. My life feels right with you, and only you. It has always been that way, and always will be."

David drew in a long breath and held it. He was thinking, hard, and when he let the breath out a small smile emerged on his lips. "Funny. I'd been thinking the very same thing while I stayed at my mom's and dad's."

I pulled back, surprised, though I shouldn't have been. David had a relationship with his parents that I envied.

"That's where you went?" I asked. "Your parents' house?"

He nodded. "Had a long talk with them, too." Then he shuddered. "Though it was really more of a lecture. Do parents ever stop doing that?"

"I don't think so," I said with a small smile of my own. "But you should feel grateful you have parents who love you enough to still give you one, David."

He glanced at me and grimaced.

"I see many clients who would give anything to have parents who set limits and give guidance," I told him. "It's more a blessing than a curse, believe me."

"I'm thirty years old, Lottie."

"Thirty or sixty, it doesn't matter. That's what makes it so wonderful."

I thought of Logan and Mrs. Reynolds and the empty, manipulative relationship they had shared. It was a sad situation made worse by lies and insecurity.

David unclasped his hands and sat upright. "I know I have a tendency to strong–arm you, but you know it's only because I want to protect you, right? And since your episodes started, I haven't been able to stop myself." David leveled his gaze with mine. "And I'm willing to bet that it didn't help us any. Hell, maybe it even made things worse between us. I don't know. I'm just so tired, I don't know what to think anymore."

David may have not have known what to think but I did. In fact, I couldn't stop thinking about Bakari's sword and what may or may not have happened that night thousands of years ago. It was the last memory I had, where time from bygone, bittersweet days ended and my second life began.

The reason for David's protective nature was more than clear.

"I think I understand why you want to safeguard me," I said. "And, in all honesty, it's not something I want you to change."

David took my hand, laced his fingers through mine and studied them with an expression that bordered on fascination, as if he'd never seen them linked together before.

"Letting you go was probably the hardest thing I've ever done," he admitted. "As much as I hoped you'd come back, I tried imagining a life where you didn't and I couldn't do it."

"I know you were thinking about moving out, though."

His head came up and his tone, along with his expression, turned somber. "For a while, I was."

"But not anymore?"

David shook his head. "No. What's happened between us—" He stopped, taking the time to think about what he wanted to say. "We have a lot of work ahead of us, you know."

Of course I knew. I'd allowed mistrust and doubt to enter our relationship, not to mention another man. And Galen's appearance in my life exposed new issues between David and me that would, eventually, have to be addressed. It was going to be a challenging road ahead.

"I'm willing to work at us," I told him. "Are you prepared to start over again, too?"

David thought about it and for a moment I had a feeling he might be reconsidering. "I think I'd prefer to pick up where we left off."

He leaned in and kissed me, and warmth spread through

me like a gentle summer breeze. Tender, inviting, and perfect.

He moved in, ready to kiss me again, and stopped. "I almost forgot," he said, reaching around and grabbing something from my nightstand. It was black and silver and the size of a tiny watch battery, and he held it up carefully between a thumb and forefinger. "I found this tucked inside the corner of the baseboard heating."

"Is this what I think it is?"

He nodded. "A listening device."

I tried taking it from David to get a better look but David pulled it away. "Careful. I'm sure this has prints."

"What on earth were you doing looking inside the baseboard?" I asked.

"I wasn't looking for anything. I was exhausted when I got home tonight and went right to bed. When I grabbed the television remote, something in the corner of the room reflected the light from the screen and I checked it out."

He placed the device back on the nightstand.

"I think that's how Mrs. Reynolds heard our conversation last Friday," he went on. "It's inactive now because I busted it, but Nat thinks it was controlled remotely from a computer."

"Mrs. Reynolds has never been to our bedroom," I said. "There's no way she'd have been able to set this in place. Besides, the person who called me was a man, not a woman."

"I thought about that, and there are only two other people who could have done this." David gave me a pointed look. "Logan or Paul."

"It was Paul," I said over a sigh. "I know in my heart that it was him. The listening device, the envelope and the hair. All of it. He'd stop by sometimes while you were away on missions and could have very easily slipped into our bedroom without me knowing it. And as a psychiatrist, he'd have access to all kinds of people to help him get the job done."

David squeezed my hand. "I'm sorry he hurt you. I know how important he was to you."

It took a lot for David to admit that, about a man he'd hated through two lifetimes. I swallowed down my grief and felt tears start to burn in my eyes. Recovering from Paul's deceit was not going to be easy.

"So should we hand over the listening device to the police, too?" I asked.

"Definitely. And we'll do that tomorrow." David edged in closer. "I have other plans for tonight."

My eyebrows arched at the suggestiveness in his words. "Oh?"

"Yes." David brushed my hair away and pressed his mouth to my neck. His breath felt warm, his lips hotter, and I tilted my head, giving him better access. "Did you know this is going to be a great night to watch the Perseid meteors?"

My interest faltered. Those weren't the plans I'd expected him to offer. "Uh, no I didn't."

His mouth moved up to my ear. He slipped my tee from my shoulder, slid down the bra strap, and dropped another kiss there. "Remember when we used to bring a blanket and cheap wine to the beach, hide away in that area behind the dunes, and watch the stars?"

I did. And I remembered doing that with Bakari, too.

I shivered under David's touch and whispered, "We didn't only watch the stars."

"I know, and I say we do it again. Tonight."

At the rate David was seducing and I was responding, I wasn't sure we'd make it past the bedroom door. "You mean now?"

"Yes." He tugged the tee down even lower.

"Seriously?"

"Yes."

"Well, I guess we could, but…" I sighed when David slid his hand underneath the tee and his fingers brushed across my stomach. "We need to get the blanket," I said, and his hand started moving upward. "And we need the wine."

David stopped.

"What's wrong?" I panted. "Why did you stop?"

He pulled back with a sheepish look on his face.

"David?" I asked again, now starting to worry. "What's wrong?"

He hesitated, like he was about to admit something he didn't want to confess. "I sort of snagged a couple of bottles from my parents' wine cellar today."

I leaned in, not sure I'd heard right. "You what?"

The sheepish look disappeared and conviction moved into its place. "I stole wine from my parents this afternoon, and I don't know why I did it."

It took a few seconds for the message to register. Then I burst out laughing, remembering how Bakari used to steal wine all the time. "David," I said, cupping his face with my hands and planting a kiss on his lips, "that is probably the most perfect thing you've said to me tonight."

His brows knit together.

"Never mind," I told him, adjusting my shirt into place and feeling charged with renewed enthusiasm. If David stole wine, then it only made sense that we ended our night by the water, too.

I told him to get himself back together and meet me downstairs. Halfway to the bedroom door, David grabbed me and stopped me. When I turned and faced him, his bright gaze seized mine and, in those peaceful seconds that passed between us, what I saw in their depths made my heart stutter. He leaned in and kissed me with softness, tenderness, and promise.

Soon after, we sat in David's packed SUV and headed for the beach, ditching our sneakers to make our way over cool, dry sand beneath a flawless, brilliant night sky. In the distance, waves thundered and crashed to the shore, and far to our right I spotted a campfire near the shoreline surrounded by dozens of people dancing and singing.

David maneuvered us into the dunes, spread out the blankets and set down two bottles of wine. I settled onto the blanket and stared up at the star–dotted sky. David followed.

"You know," David said, "the ancient people used to think the stars were their gods."

"Sirius, in particular, was an important star for them," I added.

"Yeah, I heard something like that recently. A show on NatGeo, I think."

We fell into silence, letting ourselves become enamored with the beauty stretched out before us. A meteor streaked across the sky.

"David," I said. "Do you ever think about second chances?"

Another meteor shot through the darkness. A warm breeze rustled over the tall, wild grass that blocked blowing sand and hid us from curious eyes.

He shrugged. "Sometimes." When he realized my question wasn't as innocent as it seemed, he turned to me. "Why?"

"I've been thinking. About us." In his eyes I saw the moon's reflection and something more. Something meant only for me. "Maybe it's time we started talking about making us more permanent."

David's lingering stillness was broken by the sound of the crashing waves, and it compelled me into explaining further.

"I'm not saying I want to plan a specific date. Or get a ring right this minute. But, well, I think I'm open to the idea of talking about it."

David didn't look so certain. "What changed your mind?"

"It wasn't a what. It was a who."

His brows rose. "Galen?"

I nodded.

"This guy's full of all kinds of surprises."

"And then some."

David did a double take. "Does this mean we'd have to invite him to the wedding we haven't discussed, which hasn't been discussed yet because of the engagement we haven't discussed, but that could happen sometime soon before I'm fifty?"

"Very funny." I jabbed him in the ribs. "And I think it all depends on what kind of relationship you have with him."

David pressed his lips together.

"You're not going to admit him to your team," I said, reading into his expression.

"Actually," David said, leaning back on his elbows so he could look up at the stars, "I'm going to meet with him tomorrow to discuss this again."

"Really? What changed your mind? I thought you were looking for any excuse to shut Galen down, and I figured I was the excuse to do it."

David shrugged. "I realized I was initially biased against him for no reason. Didn't think that was fair. So I'm going to give him another shot. I can't be a good commander if I let my personal life mix in with my professional one."

"You weren't biased against him for no reason, David. Instinct and intuition, even feelings of déjà vu, are powerful behaviors that shouldn't be ignored. I learned that valuable lesson myself."

David kept staring at the velvety night sky. "Is that why this feels right? Sitting by the water, drinking wine, and watching meteors?"

I leaned back on my elbows so I could study the heavens, too. "David, you have no idea how very right this is."

We didn't say anything more after that. We simply sat on the blankets, sharing wine and admiring the dark, star–dotted sky. By the time we opened the second bottle and darkness descended completely, the Perseid meteors lit up a spectacular show. David pulled me on top of him, slid off my clothes, and molded the two of us together. His skin felt hot, his body ready, and when he slid inside me we both stilled.

The moonlight caressed David's jaw and mouth and cheekbones, and played up his intense, green eyes. In those precious moments, I swore it was Bakari who looked up at me instead, like he'd done that night before he left for war. The war that had changed and sealed our fates forever.

"From childhood you have been everything to me," he

whispered. "Only now, more so. For all of eternity, you will be here, Shemei."

He pressed my hand to his heart.

Epilogue

Four Days Later
Valley of the Nobles, Egypt

Dr. Constance Arroyo stood, hands on hips, waiting, watching, and sweating.

It was damned hot in the tomb, and probably nearing one hundred twenty degrees. It was a dark place, illuminated only by the lanterns she and her team took down with them, not to mention cramped and stuffy. Not surprising, considering the tomb had been sealed off for thousands of years with passages that could accommodate no more than two people. She swiped the sweat off her brow and rubbed her dusty, dirty shirtsleeve over her forehead, desperate for water and fresh air, but she wasn't going to take a break now. She and her team were too close.

Three other workmen, dressed in jeans and tees and sneakers, kept at the digging, handing off baskets of sand to women who tag–teamed them up the passageway and out of the dig, and then down the hill and away from the excavation. Constance had come to this site, just off the banks of the Nile and deep within the Valley of the Nobles, about a year ago, working with another team on another excavation. On gut instinct and a stumble, she found an inconsistency in the rock formation near the previous dig that hinted of something beneath the surface. She'd kept her suspicions to herself and contacted her mentor, and then used all the money in her trust to buy her way inside, pay to keep mouths shut, purchase security, and fund her excavation.

Now, she stood moments away from the truth—a previously looted tomb or one that would etch her name in the history books. It was a moment every Egyptologist dreamed of.

Crouched over, because there was no room in this part of the excavation to stand at full height, Constance watched the workmen. If they didn't find an entrance soon, she might have to reconsider the position of her dig. They'd been at this for far too long and with little to show for it. And then money would start running out, and her workers would no longer want to—

"A door! A door!"

The worker's voice startled Constance into action. Grabbing a lantern and a brush, she shoved her way in between and confirmed the find. It was the outline of an entrance, a sealed mud brick door and a hieroglyphic warning that certain death would rise up and destroy anyone who dared to enter.

"Break through!" Constance ordered her team in Arabic. "Carefully! Very carefully!"

She watched as the men vigilantly chiseled their way through the entry, and soon the mud brick wall gave way. Constance coughed over the debris, aimed her lantern toward the chamber just beyond, and gasped at what she saw.

Hieroglyphs and wall paintings in red and blue, black and white, yellow and brown. Chairs made of ebony and mother of pearl. A wooden chariot. Another sealed doorway on the far wall. And gold. Lots and lots of gold.

But it wasn't the gold that captured Constance's attention.

It was the double–sized red granite sarcophagus that sat centered in the room.

"Get the crowbars!" she ordered her men. "And be careful where you walk! Nothing should be broken. Leave everything in its place for cataloguing."

It took six men to heave the three–inch lid from the sarcophagus. Constance bit her nails, alternating between watching the workers push and shove and trying to occupy herself with the hieroglyphic messages on the walls. But she couldn't concentrate. A sarcophagus this size was unheard of, not to mention ever found.

The lid finally gave way.

Constance gasped and fell to her knees once she saw her find of a lifetime. A double inner coffin, nearly five feet wide and six feet long, made of solid gold and inlaid with lapis, coral, and ebony. It was molded with the outline of a man and a woman—his eyes green, her eyes dark—and carved with ceremonial hieroglyphs. Their hands, she noted, were intertwined. On them, their names.

Constance read them out loud.

Bakari, General to Pharaoh.

Shemei, Royal Sister to Pharaoh.

"There is more," one of the workers said, pointing to hieroglyphs that covered the area over General Bakari's heart.

"Indeed, there is," Constance said, and continued to read.

From childhood to eternity

You are everything

From this life into the next

Our second chance at life and love

"Husband and wife, perhaps," Constance said.

She rose to her feet and started scanning the hieroglyphs, now better able to pick out the familiar references to Shemei and Bakari. She saw images of friendship and love, riches and royalty, triumph and sadness. She saw other images of another man, and glyphs hinting of a dark, sorrowful night during which Bakari was forced to use his jeweled sword.

The sword, Constance noticed, was resting against the tomb's farthest wall beside another image of Bakari and Shemei together, with the shadow of the other man standing just behind them.

Constance shoved her hands into her pockets and evaluated the tomb, one final look–through before the tedious job of cataloguing began.

"I wonder what Shemei's and Bakari's story is to tell," she said to no one in particular.

Then she grabbed her brush and notebook, determined to find it.

A NOTE FROM THE AUTHOR

I look for any opportunity to make stuff up. I think anything that can't so easily be explained is worth an extra look and often makes a great story. I love red wine, scotch, sunrises, Ancient Egypt, the beach—and a host of other stuff that would take too much real estate to talk about. The youngest of five children, I live with my husband and son on Long Island. And, in my next life, if I haven't moved on to somewhere else, I want to be an astronomer. I'm fascinated with the night skies almost as much as I'm fascinated with ancient Egypt.

I'm a member of member of Sisters in Crime and Mystery Writers of America, and you can read about me at http://terriponce.com/.

If you love social media, you can also find me on Facebook at https://www.facebook.com/Terri.Ponce.Author and on Twitter at https://twitter.com/TerriPonce. Come visit. I'd love to hear from you!

I truly hope you enjoyed this book you're holding in your hands. It was truly a book from the heart.

All my very best,
Terri

PS – be sure to check out Book Two of the Past Life Series, COVET. The story continues…

COVET
Book Two of the Past Life Series
~a sneak peek~

Chapter One

I'm not a guy who plays games but right now I felt like a knight on a chessboard. Moving strategically but unable to set up for checkmate. It wasn't that my patterns were ineffective. It was that fate had decided to throw an extra playing piece on the board.

"She's going to make a move," Galen said.

I'd seen the woman he was referring to from the corner of my eye, watching me. The problem was, she wasn't my target. I downed my beer and ordered another from the bartender. He was juggling two martinis, some pink girly drink, and a white wine while someone at the other end of the bar whined about being cut off. I momentarily wondered if life as a bartender might be a lot simpler and immediately dismissed the thought. I thrived on excitement. That's why I was here, senses alert, adrenalin pumping, on the edge. Ready. And if it got dangerous…well, I was ready for that, too.

"I'm telling you, Bellotti," Galen said. "She's interested. More than interested."

This was going to be a problem. I took the fresh draft from the bartender, slid him a bunch of Euros, and watched the woman through the reflection in the mirror behind the bar. Not bad but I wasn't interested. I'd already committed to the best.

Back home.

"Concentrate on the op," I said, lowering my voice.

The music pounded in the adjoining, jammed dance floor. People boozed it up and snorted stuff I didn't want to know about in dark corners of Istanbul's hottest nightclub.

I buried myself in my beer, keeping true to my cover. "We have a job to do," I told Galen. "No distractions."

We were to surveil a local drug dealer, Zev Sahin. Local for Turkey. Not local for Galen and me. I looked the Italian-American tourist, but Galen—a native Australian—somehow inherited Middle Eastern features. That made moving around the country a little easier. The nightclub was top-grade and the food and drink were covered by PROs, the professional military corporation we worked for, and if everything went as planned, in two days the op would be a wrap and I'd be vacationing back home with the love of my life.

Loud laughter broke out at a nearby table and I used the pulsating lights that illuminated the dance floor to scan the nightclub again. I watched the dealer, careful not to draw attention to myself. He sat on a sofa set back in a dark corner, surrounded by women, beefy bodyguards, and empty bottles of Cristal. And I waited for the lynch pin—the person who was going to set the wheels in motion for the night.

"She's playing with her hair and she's staring at you, Bellotti. I think she's going to make a move soon."

"Wipe that grin off your face or I'll do it for you," I told Galen.

"I'm just waiting for the fireworks." Galen laughed as he picked up his glass. "What line are you going to use this time? You have an arsenal that always seems to piss off women."

"I don't piss them off," I said. "They just aren't used to honesty. Which doesn't say a whole lot for relationships or dating these days, does it?"

Galen shrugged. "I think you're jaded. You walk in with attitude and Armani, turn heads, and then moan about the unwanted attention you get."

I studied the two of us in the mirror, both in designer clothes, both trying to blend in with the upscale crowd. Only Galen didn't have the harshness on his face that I did. People probably looked at me tonight and saw someone who wanted to break a face. In reality, it was exhaustion. I really needed that damned vacation.

"You're making too big a deal out of this," I said.

I was going to say more but stopped when I saw our lynch pin walk into the club. She positioned herself near a granite column off to the side of the dance floor, all long legs, blonde hair, and killer body in a tight blue dress.

Lady in Blue slinked through the crowd, every man's head turning as she moved. Galen stilled and said, "Wow."

"We're a go," I said, setting down the beer. I glanced at Sahin once more through the mirror's reflection.

"Do you think this will work?" Galen asked.

"It has to. If we're to get into Zev Sahin's compound and warehouse, we need that keycard he keeps in his wallet. His weak spot for women will get us that card."

"Poor damned SOB has no idea what's coming," Galen said as Lady in Blue moved in. Then he sighed, had a little more of the vodka he'd been nursing, and shrugged it off. "You realize that this will be the easy part compared to getting him to turn."

"That's not our problem," I reminded him, staring him down. Galen knew it was all about the rest of our team, the DEA, and the U.S. Government. All we had to do was get the card after the wallet was lifted and make the drop, and then the rest of our guys would get into the warehouse and take it down. After that, we stepped out of the picture.

And my vacation with Lottie began. With brisk walks on the beach, huddling in a warm blanket, and relaxing with a bottle of red. I shook my head. Who the hell was I kidding? I intended to keep Lottie in bed for a whole week.

"Do you think it will be that easy?" Galen asked.

I grinned, knowing Lottie wanted that week in bed, too. "Damned straight."

"I hope you're right."

I realized Galen was talking about the op and that I'd let my mind wander. Not good. In this business, distraction led to death.

"She's moving in, Bellotti," Galen said.

Lady in Blue strode toward Sahin, bending over to adjust the strap on her high-heeled shoe, giving him enough bare leg and bare breast to catch his attention. It worked. Sahin smiled at her and beckoned her over with a bottle of Cristal. She cocked her head, giving him just enough coy to reel him in.

A warm body brushed against my arm. I ignored it, watching the way Lady in Blue moved and keeping Sahin just inside my field of vision. A hand settled on my bicep and squeezed. It was the woman who had been trying to get my interest.

"Hi," she said, a smile on her face and in her voice.

"Hi," I said, not smiling at all.

"My name is Yvette." She was decked out in red hair and red dress, and was now officially baggage. "Mind if I join you?" She pulled up a spare barstool between Galen and me.

Past Yvette, Lady in Blue nuzzled onto Sahin's lap. Sahin snagged a waitress, said something to her, and stuffed a wad of Euros down her cleavage. She strutted away, happy with the fat tip.

Yvette snuggled onto the barstool, blocking my view.

"Yvette," I said firmly, "I'm not looking for company."

"Oh." She seemed put off at first but quickly recovered. I got the feeling I'd just become a challenge and she leaned in closer. C-cups, pressed hard against my arm.

That gave me a clear view of the action again. Lady in Blue slipped her arms around Sahin, slid off his jacket, and ran her hands over his chest and stomach. Good. All she had to do next was distract him the way only a woman like her could, snatch the wallet, and pretend to break outside for a smoke, where I'd meet her to make the exchange.

"You're the hottest guy in here," Yvette said, leaning in and giving me a clear view of a nicely filled red and black bra. "You alone?"

Galen tapped the bar to get my attention and flicked his eyes to a position behind him. His six o'clock.

My gaze slid past Yvette's other shoulder. Another woman, dressed in a black pantsuit, stood at the entrance to the dance floor where Lady in Blue had been earlier. Only this woman's body language said she was ready to kill, and I immediately knew who the victim would be.

It was Sahin's wife. I looked back at Yvette. "I saw you making the moves on that Navy guy over there," and I jerked my head to where he sat with a bunch of his friends.

She looked at him then looked back at me. "I'm not interested in him."

"Yeah." I grinned. "But I am."

Yvette's mouth opened and stayed that way.

"Should we move in?" Galen asked.

Yvette shoved away, probably thinking Galen was talking about the Navy guy.

I watched Sahin's wife weave through the crowd to her husband, whose head was buried in Lady in Blue's breasts. One of his bodyguards saw the wife coming and tapped Sahin's shoulder. Sahin ignored him.

Sahin's wife stood, hands on hips, staring down at her husband. Then, without warning, she picked up a bottle of Cristal and slammed it on the table and started screaming. She took another and smashed it on the floor, then another. The loud *pops* startled the crowd, someone yelled "she's got a gun!" and the place went berserk. People scrambled to get out, shoving off the dance floor, jamming into the doorways, and screaming for safety. Bouncers pushed against the tide of patrons, yelling for them to calm down, and rounding them up like cattle.

Sahin barked at his wife in Turkish. His wife lunged for Lady in Blue and swung at her with another bottle. Lady in Blue dodged the attack, a foot slid out from under her, and she went down, her head clipping the coffee table. She didn't move.

"Watch my back," I told Galen.

"I'll go after Blue," he said. "You get that wallet."

I nodded and took off.

Sahin argued with his wife, surrounded by the bodyguards. I moved in fast, knowing I had one shot at this. Screw it up and I blew my cover. Succeed and I still had a career. I strode toward the group of them, eyes on Lady in Blue but my mind on that wallet. One of the bodyguards slammed a hand to my chest, stopping me. He said something in Turkish that I didn't understand, but I got the message. I wasn't getting any closer.

"She's hurt," I said, pointing a finger to our spook on the floor. "She needs help."

I made to move in again but the guy put a gun to my head. I stared at him, calm on the outside, heart pounding within. I held my hands up in surrender. No need to piss him off. Let him think he had me. I just needed another plan.

Galen was one step ahead of me. He muscled his way in to Lady in Blue, distracting the bodyguards. The gun that was on me swung to Galen. I grabbed Sahin's jacket, swiped the wallet, and threw the jacket back on the chair. I kept going, not breaking stride, slipping the wallet into my pocket. I didn't look back.

I was almost at the door when a gun fired, followed by a heavily accented shout. "Stop him! Stop him!"

I blew out the entrance and took off, hustling through the panicked crowd. Another gun fired and police sirens sounded in the distance. I made a left down a small street then a right into an alley, jumping a garbage can, hurtling over a short wall, and disappearing into the neighborhood. If Galen didn't make it to our backup rendezvous point, I had to get to the safe house and that was five miles away. And right now, I had no idea if Galen and Lady in Blue were still alive.

I skidded past a corner, wondering if I should take the

chance and call an alert into HQ, when I heard screeching tires. I backed up, pressed myself against a wall, and realized who it was. Galen in a Toyota. He threw open the passenger door and I jumped in, slamming the door shut as Galen jammed the gas pedal.

"You get it?" he asked, swerving through a turn then dropping our speed so we didn't draw attention.

I nodded. "Is Lady in Blue okay?"

Galen hugged another turn. "She will be. She came to when the gunshots were fired."

I blew out a sigh of relief. It wasn't the first time a distraction job had taken a bad turn, but it was still a worry. "And the cops?"

"All at the nightclub. But we will have to lose the car." He used his cell phone and dialed our contact, making arrangements for cleanup.

I pulled out Sahin's wallet and lifted the keycard. "Payday," I said, holding it up.

"Mommie Dearest says we should leave the wallet and card with the car." Galen disconnected the call. "They will pick it all up at the Starbucks near the safe house in ten minutes."

I drew in a breath and held it, forcing my heart and my lungs to calm down. Another close call. I loved this shit.

"You love this shit *way too much*," Galen said, glancing my way.

I had known Galen all of three months, and he was far too good at reading my mind already. I was trying to get my head wrapped around the fact that we were connected in a way that didn't make sense, but that didn't mean I had to like it. Ignoring him, I sank into the seat, letting the adrenalin wear off.

"Let's see what else we've got on this guy." Inside his wallet I found a black American Express, a MasterCard, and over five thousand Euros in the billfold. A picture was tucked in with his identification. I pulled it out and held it up to catch the light from passing street lamps.

It was a photo of the love of my life kissing another man.

~~~

30988408R00153

Printed in Great Britain
by Amazon